THE SHADOW AT GREYSTONE CHASE

An Angela Marchmont Mystery Book 10

CLARA BENSON

MOUNT STREET PRESS

MOUNT
STREET
PRESS

Copyright

© 2015 Clara Benson

ISBN: 978-1-913355-09-8

The right of Clara Benson to be identified as the author
of this work has been asserted by her in accordance with
the Copyright, Designs and Patents Act, 1988

ClaraBenson.com

Cover design by Shayne Rutherford at
wickedgoodbookcovers.com

Interior Design & Typesetting by Ampersand Book Interiors
ampersandbookinteriors.com

CHAPTER ONE

M RS. ANGELA MARCHMONT was not a woman who liked to admit weakness. Having worked hard and overcome numerous obstacles—not least the inconvenient fact of her sex—to achieve material success, she had, over the years, found it politic to adopt a serene and cheery demeanour which was intended to convey the impression of a person who was not easily daunted, and who could be relied upon to undertake any task with little fuss and a reasonable degree of competence. As time went on, this outward appearance became so natural to her that it grew to be quite a habit, and she had found it so useful on various occasions that she saw no reason to abandon it. So convincing was she that many people—including some of her closest friends—assumed that she really was as permanently sanguine and untroubled as she seemed, and Angela never bothered to disabuse them of the notion, for she had discovered that there were decided benefits to be had from the ability to present an unruffled façade to the world at large. True, there were some who considered her a little cool—unfeeling, even—but since Angela was also happily possessed of a great deal of personal charm, those people tended to be in the minority. The majority, meanwhile, took her smiles at face value, and it never occurred to them to wonder whether there might be anything more below the surface than that which she chose to display above it.

Following her trial for the murder of her husband, Angela, true to character, resolved to put the events of the past winter behind her as soon as she could, and was determined never to reveal to a soul how bruised and battered she had been by the whole experience. To that end, she immediately accepted every invitation she received from her many concerned friends, who were in unanimous agreement that she ought to leave London for a while—at least until the days grew longer and memories began to fade. Angela was more touched by their kindness than she could say, for she had been uncertain of how they would react to the revelations which had come out in court about her past. It is not everyone who is prepared to take with equanimity the discovery that a friend has been concealing the existence of an illegitimate child for fourteen years, and Angela was not entirely surprised to discover that there were some whose affection for her cooled markedly after the event. Still, she was by no means a pariah, and so she put on a brave face and affected not to notice the defection of those who had decided they wanted nothing more to do with her. This was partly for her daughter's sake, for now that Barbara knew the truth Angela was determined to do right by her, and therefore firmly refused to give any indication that she might be at all ashamed of the girl. Barbara had already lost quite enough because of her mother's mistakes, and the last thing she needed was to feel as though Angela did not want her now that there was no longer any good reason for them to be apart.

Between social engagements, therefore, Angela took care to visit Barbara at school as often as she could without causing embarrassment, and to write at least twice a week, and as far as she could tell (although who knew what went on in the mind of a fourteen-year-old girl?) Barbara was happy with the new arrangement. Angela knew her daughter well enough to be fairly certain that if there were anything to complain about, she would hear about it soon enough, and so after a few months her anxiety began to lessen and she started to believe that perhaps she was not *quite* the worst mother in the world, which had been her firmest conviction up to then. A little to her surprise, she found herself enjoying Barbara's company more and more, and had some ado to suppress her self-reproach at having left things so long. Barbara was kind enough not to mention it, however, and Angela hoped that the guilt would wear off in time.

So the months passed, and spring came and went. Since February Angela had spent two weeks in the South of France, a week in Bournemouth, and various weekends in Hampshire, Somerset and Leicestershire. She had attended the races three times and been hunting once. In April she went sailing and in May attended a flower show. She also visited her brother and his wife in Surrey—an uncomfortable experience in which they all did their best not to mention the trial, and Humphrey went into agonies over whether or not he ought to acknowledge the existence of his hitherto unsuspected niece. Angela had already departed before he made his decision, and in a fever of guilt he sent a letter after her in which he meant to indicate his support (although not his approval), but which was full of such tortuous language and flowery expression that it would have conveyed nothing to anyone who did not know him as well as his sister did. Angela smiled when she received it, and appreciated his intentions, but decided not to visit again for a long while.

Thus was she kept busy. She was not tactless enough to throw herself into the usual round of gaiety, evening-parties and night-clubs, for although she was not at all sorry at her husband's death, Angela was fully aware of the hypocrisy which was required of her, and so she was careful to accept only invitations to the more muted sorts of engagement, at which she put on a brisk manner that was intended to discourage anyone from asking too many questions. Of course, it would have been unnatural to refuse to talk about the thing at all, and so whenever the conversation floated in that direction (as it invariably did sooner or later), and someone asked a hesitant question as to how she was, Angela replied with a smile, and agreed that yes, it had all been dreadful, but that she was doing her best to forget it now. Something about the way she replied tended to discourage further inquiry, but occasionally someone of little perception would venture further and say how fortunate it was that they had caught the *real* murderer in the end, and at that moment Angela would nod and change the subject abruptly, and nothing more would be said about it.

Hardly anyone knew the real truth about what had happened that day in court, and Angela had no intention of enlightening them. It was an uncomfortable feeling, to say the least, to owe one's life to a man for whom one had harboured a guilty— infatuation, she supposed it must be called (for she would not dignify it with a higher name), and who had turned out to have done something unspeakable. Angela was disgusted at herself for her own stupidity in having been drawn in by Edgar Valencourt, who had killed his wife, but she hated herself even more for the terrible lie she had told in court, which had allowed him to take the blame for her husband's murder onto his own shoulders. Even though it had been the only way out for her, and he had fully meant her to do it, she knew she had done him a great wrong, and she struggled daily with her conscience, for it did not do to pin a crime on an innocent man, however bad he was in other respects. Still, it was all too late now; he was dead and the thing was over and done with, and Angela was determined that nobody should ever know of her broken heart, for she felt she did not deserve pity.

She therefore put on her usual cheerful face and went about her business, and no-one could have guessed that she was anything other than tremendously relieved at her acquittal and keen to return to normal life as far as possible. True, she was thinner than she had been, and perhaps she laughed a little less, but not so much as to be especially obvious. She slept badly these days, too, but the dark circles under her eyes were easy enough to conceal with a touch of make-up. Only Marthe, her faithful maid, observed the hours Angela spent staring out of the window apparently unseeing; noticed, too, her mistress's increased absent-mindedness, which meant a question often had to be repeated two or three times before it would be answered. She also knew that Angela had taken to rising early and going for restless walks, although on her return she often could not say where she had been. Marthe saw all this and worried for her mistress's health, but Angela dismissed her concerns and said she was perfectly well.

It was towards the end of May when Angela returned to her flat in Mount Street one evening, after having spent several days with some friends in Oxfordshire. These days the flat had the tidy, empty appearance of someone who lived in it little, and the post tended to pile up. Angela glanced through the heap of correspondence which awaited her attention.

'I seem to be running up rather a lot of bills lately,' she remarked, as Marthe busied herself with the luggage. 'Now, if I were as respectable as I ought to be, I should have a nice, stuffy, middle-aged husband, who would regard me sorrowfully over his spectacles as I prostrated myself at his feet and confessed my profligacy, and then pay them all for me with a sigh.'

Marthe's wrinkled nose indicated quite clearly what she thought of that.

'Oh, an invitation from the Atchisons,' said Angela, reading. 'They want me to go to Edinburgh on Thursday. Do we want to go to Scotland? It's a long way and he's rather a bore. Perhaps I'll say no this time. What else? A postcard from Barbara to say that she *almost* passed the French exam, whatever that means. Now, what's this?' she went on, opening another letter, whose postmark and appearance indicated it as being of a legal nature. 'Don't tell me Mr. Addison has found something else to charge me for. It's quite extraordinary how they manage to bill one for things that one might have supposed were included in the service—'

Here she broke off, for the letter was not from Mr. Addison at all. Marthe glanced up in curiosity at Angela's sudden silence, and raised her eyebrows at the sight of her mistress's face, which had assumed a blank, closed expression.

'What is it?' she asked.

Angela did not reply, but continued to stare at the single sheet of paper in her hand. Its letterhead declared it to be from a firm of solicitors by the name of Gilverson and Gilverson, and it read simply:

Friday, 17th May

Dear Mrs. Marchmont,

I write in respect of my late client, Edgar Valencourt de Lisle, about whom I have a communication to make that would be better discussed in private. I should therefore be very grateful if you would come to my office at your earliest convenience. Might I suggest next Friday, 24th May, at 2 p.m? If not, I shall be more than happy to accommodate any other day you prefer.

Yours sincerely,
Charles Gilverson

P.S: *Please be assured that all discussions will re-main absolutely confidential.*

Angela gazed at the wall for a few moments, looked back at the letter to remind herself of the date suggested for the appointment with Charles Gilverson, thought for an instant and reached a sudden decision.

'Go and send a telegram to the Atchisons and tell them we'll be there on Thursday,' she said to Marthe. 'And you'd better start looking up the train times.'

'But I thought you did not wish to go,' said Marthe.

'I've changed my mind,' said Angela, in a tone that brooked no argument.

Marthe went off to do as she was bid. When she had gone, Angela drummed her fingers vigorously on the mantelpiece for some two minutes. She then took up the letter, read it once more, crumpled it up and threw it in the waste-paper basket. After another minute she fished it out and tore it into pieces for good measure. She had no idea what this Charles Gilverson wanted to say to her, but it could not possibly be anything she wanted to hear. Perhaps there had been a mistake. At any rate, she had no intention of going to his office, and of course he would not have the temerity to try again. She would ignore the summons and go to Scotland instead, and then he would go away and leave her alone.

CHAPTER TWO

BUT IF ANGELA thought she could escape the inevitable, she was wrong. She spent a very dull week in Scotland and returned to London, secure in the knowledge that she had missed her appointment with Mr. Gilverson and thus had nothing to fear. To her dismay, therefore, the first thing she saw when Marthe presented her with her post was a familiar-looking envelope, addressed to her in the same hand as the first letter, but bigger and bulkier this time. Evidently this one contained more than just a single sheet of paper.

'That will be all,' said Angela pointedly to Marthe, who was hovering about with an expression of the strongest curiosity. Marthe stuck out her chin and reluctantly withdrew, and Angela opened the envelope with some trepidation. Inside was a letter and another, smaller envelope addressed to her. She turned her attention to the letter first. It was from Mr. Gilverson, and it read:

Wednesday, 29th May

Dear Mrs. Marchmont,

It has occurred to me that my earlier letter may have come as something of an unwelcome surprise to you in view of the unfortunate events that occurred last winter, about which I imagine you hardly want to be reminded. If it did, then I beg your pardon. My intention was never to upset or alarm you in any way, and I hope you will forgive me if I have inadvertently done so. I wrote to you originally in fulfilment of instructions left to me by my late client, who asked me to communicate with you a certain number of months after his death. He did not specify how many months, but he was clear in his wish that you be given time to recover from your ordeal before I wrote to you.

Having reflected upon the situation, and since I understand the enclosed letter is somewhat personal in nature, I have now decided to send it to you directly, in order to allow you to read it in private and consider the course of action you wish to take, if any. My client referred to your generosity of spirit several times during our conversation, and was hopeful that you would be prevailed upon to lend your assistance in resolving his problem. However, since it is by rights his own concern and none of yours, please be assured that no recrimination of any kind will be due to you should you decide to decline; on the contrary, I am aware of the demands I am placing upon you even by writing to you now, and you therefore have my word that if I do not hear from you, this is the last communication you will receive from me regarding this matter.

If there is anything further you wish to know, I can be communicated with at any time at the above address.

I remain,
Yours sincerely,
Charles Gilverson

Angela hardly knew what she had been expecting—a blackmail demand had been her immediate assumption on receiving the first letter—but this was a surprise indeed. What could it mean? She now turned to the smaller envelope and regarded it warily. It bore only her name, written in a clear, masculine hand; presumably that of the man she had known as Edgar Valencourt. Her first thought on looking at it was that his handwriting was wholly unfamiliar to her, for he had never written to her nor she to him. How little she had known him! And what *had* she known of him, after all, but what he had told her? It was not until that fateful day in court that she had found out his terrible secret and felt her world collapse about her ears. Now she hesitated for some time before opening the letter, since it seemed that no good could possibly come of it. After all, what could it be except an explanation for his conduct and a demand for her gratitude in return for his having taken the blame upon himself? He was dead now, and nothing he could say would change what had happened, so why read the letter and reopen the wounds that had begun slowly to heal over? For a few moments, indeed, she had half a mind to tear it up unread, but something stopped her and she could not bring herself to do it. She bit her lip, then at last opened the envelope reluctantly and took out the letter it contained. It was written on cheap paper she recognized well from her own time in prison, and was dated mid-January, before his escape and subsequent death at the hands of a criminal gang.

My darling Angela (it read),

I expect by now you're sick and tired of the very sound of my name, and would be quite happy never to hear it again—and believe me, I thought long and hard before putting pen to paper today, since the last thing I want is to remind you of this whole sorry business. In fact, I shouldn't blame you if you wanted to throw this letter into the fire and refuse to read it, but I know your generosity and I hope you'll be kind enough to give me your attention for just a few minutes, even if I don't deserve it.

Of course, you know how bad I've been—it's not as though I've kept it a secret from you, and it would be ridiculous of me to try and deny it now. The police have been looking for me for a long time, and with good reason. I'm a thief and a criminal and probably worse besides. I've done things that any right-thinking person would be ashamed of, and felt no remorse—at least until recently. But Angela, I'm not a murderer. I was tried and convicted, and I escaped from prison by a stroke of pure luck, but if they'd succeeded in hanging me they'd have hanged the wrong man. I spent ten years and more running away from 'justice,' as they like to call it, with no possible means of clearing my name. I was marked down as bad, and in a fit of defiance—rage—I don't know what—I went on to show them just how bad I could be. If they thought me guilty then it seemed to me that I might as well live up to the description. So that's what I did—at least until I met you. You were kind to me even though I'd deceived you, and I can't tell you how much it lifted my spirits to feel that there was one person at least who saw a little good in me, when everybody else, including myself, considered me to be wholly bad.

Now I'd like to ask you to be kind to me one last time. I've never been one to abandon hope, and it seems to me that you're the only one I have left, so I'm afraid I'm going to be terribly selfish once again and ask for your help. Selina did not die at my hands. Of that, at least, I'm completely innocent. I don't expect you to believe my word, of course—the police didn't, after all—but I should be so very obliged if you would consider taking a little time to look into the matter yourself and to come to your own conclusions. I was found guilty on quite circumstantial evidence, and I should like as much as anyone for the real culprit to be brought to justice. It oughtn't to matter, but while I'm still alive to care about it, I'd like to think there was a chance that one day this particular stain on my character might be removed.

I know there's nothing you can do to help me now—that's not what I'm asking, and in fact I've instructed Charles not to communicate with you until after my death. You've had quite enough on your own plate and it would hardly be kind of me to add to it. But I will confess to feeling comfort at the idea that someone *might be prepared to give me the benefit of the doubt long enough to try and find out what really happened that day, and I should very much like that someone to be you. I know you have a deep sense of justice, and won't be swayed by all the other things you know to my disadvantage, and I believe if anyone can discover the truth and clear my name, you can. Then perhaps one day you will come to think better of me than you do now.*

If you do decide to help me, Charles can give you all the details of the case. If you don't, then there's no harm done. For myself, I wish you every happiness.

Yours ever,
Edgar

Angela's first reaction on reading the letter was one of anger. Was it never to end? Was she never to be free of him, even after his death? How *dare* he call her darling and demand her help, as though none of the last few months had ever happened? As though he had not hidden his murderous past from her until it was revealed so dramatically that day in court? As though he had never offered himself up as a sacrifice and put her in his debt forever?

Here her anger receded as quickly as it had arisen and she sagged a little, because of course that was the *real* heart of the matter: her own deep-seated guilt at having allowed him to do it. She was less angry with him than she was with herself. She was under a great obligation to him, and they both knew it, although—drat the man—he had not been so tactless as even to hint at it in his letter. He had not asked her to return any favour, but had expressed his request merely in terms of her doing him a kindness. There was no begging or pleading, and—except for the initial endearment—no indelicate hinting at anything more than past friendship to embarrass her. Had the letter come from anyone else she would most likely have been moved to pity and agreed to the request immediately.

But why had he asked her to investigate the murder of his wife at all? Surely he must be guilty. Of course he was guilty. Why, the alternative was unthinkable, for if he really were innocent of murder then that made his sacrifice for her all the greater, and all the more incomprehensible. Just then Angela was struck by a thought which had not occurred to her before, and she drew in a sharp breath. Why had she never realized it? Of course! The reason Edgar Valencourt must have come forward and confessed to the murder of Davie Marchmont was because he believed that she had done it. There was no other explanation for it, for had he believed in the culpability of a mysterious third party then he would most likely have assumed that Angela's defence would produce some evidence of it, and that Angela would be acquitted on balance. But the fact that he had stepped in pointed to his belief that there *was* no evidence, for the real murderer was already standing there in the dock. She had told him herself that she had been frightened she might kill her husband one day, but that did not mean she had done it. On the contrary, she had run away to avoid the temptation. Davie's death had been entirely his own fault, caused by his own greed and stupidity.

At that her anger returned. She had not thought it possible to resent Edgar Valencourt any more than she already did, but the idea of his suspecting her of being as bad as himself and patronizing her with this grand gesture of his irritated her to a quite extraordinary degree. She was on the point of tearing the letter up as she had originally intended when Marthe came in with the tea things, perhaps suspecting that her mistress was in need of a restorative. Angela had no desire to work off her fit of pique before Marthe and expose herself to the girl's raised eyebrows, and so she put the letter aside and took a cup. The tea went some way to calming her temper, and on reflection she began to think that she was being somewhat irrational. Perhaps some fresh air would clear her head.

'I'm going for a walk,' she said to Marthe, and without further ado went out. In a very few minutes she was in the Park, and almost without intending it found herself drifting towards the Serpentine and the bench on which Valencourt had joined her on that fateful day all those months ago. He had told her that he was going to retire, and she had believed him—for a little while, at least. But he had had no chance to keep his promise, for later that day everything had gone horribly wrong and nothing had been the same since.

She hesitated, then sat down. The sun was shining but there was a brisk breeze which chilled the air, and Angela pulled her coat about her. A few hardy children were throwing themselves into the water with shrieks of glee and she watched them idly for a few minutes. Her anger had dissipated now, and she was merely thoughtful. Quite aside from all other considerations, after her trial she had vowed to give up detecting, for her conscience would no longer allow her to act on the side of justice when she had lied under oath in court. On the other hand, she *did* owe Valencourt an enormous debt of obligation for his having induced her to tell that lie—for there was no doubt at all that she would have been found guilty and hanged had he not done what he did. But which argument held the greater force? She wrestled with this for several minutes, hoping that some unassailable point would strike her which would demonstrate beyond all doubt that she ought to keep well out of the thing, but it was no use; her sense of fairness *would* intrude and insist that his having been prepared to give up his life for her trumped her delicacy of conscience hands down.

She sighed. If she had not known him, he had certainly known *her* well enough to be sure that she would do as he asked, if only out of a sense of duty. And yet what good could it do? He was dead now and would never know whether his name were cleared or not—and she was convinced it would not be, for surely he must be guilty. There was no doubt that he was an accomplished enough liar for his protestations of innocence to sound believable enough, but by his own admission he was a criminal, and a mostly unrepentant one at that. The investigation would be a waste of time and would result in nothing useful, she was sure of it. His request for help was just yet another way of drawing her in even after his death. And yet she must do it. Little as she liked it, it was the only way to repay her debt.

CHAPTER THREE

I AM RELIEVED to see that my first letter didn't frighten you off,' said Mr. Gilverson, as Angela took a seat. 'This is an unusual case, and it didn't occur to me until afterwards that perhaps I ought to have been a little less abrupt.'

'No, it didn't frighten me off,' lied Angela. 'The letter happened to arrive while I was away, that's all.'

'Well, it's not at all the sort of thing I am accustomed to dealing with, which is why my approach was perhaps less than sensitive, shall we say.'

'What do you usually deal with?'

'Oh, it's a very quiet practice I have here. Most of my clients are of very long standing, and come to me for wills and deeds and contracts, and that kind of thing. As a matter of fact, I shall be retiring soon and giving it all up for a life in the country.'

'How delightful,' said Angela politely. She had the oddest feeling that she had met Charles Gilverson before, and was racking her brains trying to place him. She had arrived at his office in some trepidation, still half-expecting to be confronted with his knowledge of her perjury and presented with a demand for money, but Mr. Gilverson looked in no way like a blackmailer (whatever a blackmailer looked like), and indeed had a polite and genial manner which went some way towards reassuring her that she was not about to be drawn into an unpleasant dispute of a financial nature.

'So, then, I take it my unruly nephew has managed to persuade you to look into this sorry mess,' said the solicitor. 'He always did have a way with words, although much good it did him in this case.'

'Your nephew?' said Angela in surprise. She looked more closely at Mr. Gilverson. So that was why she had thought him familiar. There was a distinct resemblance between the two, and now she saw that he had the same deep blue eyes as Valencourt. Presumably it was a family trait. The revelation did nothing to make her feel any more at ease, however.

'Yes. I am his lawyer as well as his uncle,' said Mr. Gilverson, 'although I fear his activities in later years were outside my usual sphere of expertise, and so I had rather washed my hands of him until last January, when he wrote to me from prison with this very unusual request.'

'Oh,' said Angela, nonplussed.

'Now, I shall begin by being abrupt again,' said Mr. Gilverson. 'Please understand that I did not call you here to discuss the death of your husband or the events of the trial last January. I think we may consider that matter closed, and whatever may or may not have occurred in court is not the question at hand today. I am not interested in making you uncomfortable by resurrecting the thing, so please do not worry.'

Angela took this to mean that he understood her fear of blackmail and was reassuring her, but would not allow him to labour under any misapprehension.

'Thank you,' she said. 'However, before we dispense with the subject entirely I should like to make it quite clear to you that I was not in any way responsible for my husband's death.'

She would have liked to explain further, but knew she would not come out well in the story, and so she left it at that.

'I'm glad to hear it,' said Mr. Gilverson with a smile. 'Now,' he went on briskly. 'To the present matter. As you know, in July of nineteen eighteen my nephew was put on trial for the murder of his wife. He maintained his innocence throughout, but of course, as you know only too well, the police do on occasion make mistakes, and a jury can hardly be expected to reach the correct conclusion when they are presented with only a limited set of information. The situation was not helped by the fact that he did not receive the support of his family, most of whom turned their backs on him and left him to his fate. The outcome was therefore inevitable: he was found guilty and sentenced to death. It was his good fortune that a few days before he was due to hang there was a disturbance at the prison at which he was being held, during which several prisoners escaped, including my nephew. He went on the run, as I believe they call it, and when I next heard of him, he was on the Continent and was being sought by the police for the theft of an emerald necklace and bracelet from some minor Austrian aristocrat.'

'Had he ever done anything of the sort before?' said Angela curiously.

'Not exactly,' said Mr. Gilverson. 'There were one or two scrapes in his student days, I believe, but nothing quite as serious as this. Still, it seems the life of a thief appealed to him, and he continued with it until his arrest in January of this year.'

'Didn't the police ever realize he was the same man they wanted for murder?'

'Not as far as I can tell,' said Mr. Gilverson. 'And why should they? Unlike theft, murder is not the sort of thing in which one generally engages as a career. They are two quite different types of crime. There was no reason for the police to think that Edgar de Lisle and Edgar Valencourt were one and the same. Of course, there was always the possibility that someone might see the name and put two and two together, but it seems they never did.'

'Were you in communication with him while he was on the run?'

'On occasion. Not all the time, of course, but every once in a while I would hear from him.'

'And you never told the police of his whereabouts?'

'No,' said Mr. Gilverson. 'Strange as it seems—and not that he deserved it—I was fond of my nephew, and didn't want to see him hanged. A terrible breach of ethics on the part of a solicitor, of course, but in my experience, whenever the head and the heart come into conflict, the heart wins every time.'

'That's true enough,' said Angela without thinking.

Mr. Gilverson regarded her with seeming sympathy.

'I see we understand one another,' he said.

Angela looked away, for his eyes made her uncomfortable. He went on:

'So, then, we come to last January, after my nephew turned himself in and was arrested. I visited him in prison before he escaped again, and he told me then that he thought he had found someone who might be prepared to investigate Selina's murder. I won't deny I was surprised when he gave me your name, but he seemed certain that you would be kind enough to accept his request for help.'

Angela opened her mouth to speak, but knew not what to say. She longed to know what had gone on between the two of them in prison. More must have been said than Gilverson had told her, surely. How much did the solicitor know? Obviously he knew of her acquaintance with Edgar Valencourt, in which case he must also know that she had lied about it in court. Did he believe Valencourt to be guilty of Davie's murder? It was impossible to broach the subject without everything coming out, however, and so she gave it up.

'Do you believe he murdered his wife?' she said instead.

'No, I don't,' said Mr. Gilverson.

'But the rest of his family do?'

'So one would suppose.'

Angela looked up, suddenly alert.

'What do you mean?' she said. 'Do you think they believe him innocent too? But then why should they have turned their backs on him, as you said?'

'That is a very good question,' said Mr. Gilverson. 'Yes, a very good question indeed.'

He had her curiosity now.

'You had better tell me the whole story,' she said at last.

Chapter Four

'VERY WELL,' SAID Mr. Gilverson. He laid his hands on the desk in front of him and placed his fingertips together. 'First of all, I had better tell you something about the de Lisles. The French side of the family are descended from Louis the Fourteenth—or so they claim; whether that is true or not I cannot tell you. However, what is certain is that the de Lisles were rich landowners who owned much of the wine-growing country around Rheims and developed a certain fame in France as producers of champagne. In recent years they formed alliances in the old mediaeval manner—that is, through marriage—with one or two great English families, which had the effect of increasing their fortunes considerably. The mother of Roger de Lisle, Edgar's father, was English, as was Edgar's own mother, Evelyn, and the family spent much of the time in England and in other places around the Continent.

'When the war broke out, the family left Rheims, which was too close to the front line for comfort, and decamped to Kent for the duration. Their house, Greystone Chase, had originally belonged to the English part of the family on Roger's side, and was only one of the de Lisles' many properties here and abroad, so it was merely a case of removing from one home to another. It was fortunate, in fact, that they had such a home to remove *to*, for during the war their house just outside Rheims was completely destroyed and the vineyards laid to waste.'

'Goodness,' said Angela.

'Yes, they had a lucky escape, as I understand it,' said Mr. Gilverson. 'Still, it did not prevent Roger and Evelyn de Lisle from spending the war in comfort. They lived at Greystone Chase, as did their eldest son, Godfrey, who spent most of the war in London behind a desk, since he was exempted from active service following a bout of pneumonia in his youth, which left him with weak lungs. Edgar spent some time in France on intelligence duties, although he also fought on the front line, and by all accounts served his country honourably.

'It was while he was home on leave in nineteen sixteen that Edgar met and married Selina Lacey. She was the orphan daughter of a Canterbury family, and was very young when they met. She was under the guardianship of her brother Henry, who was not much older than she and pretty much allowed her to run wild. He was certainly more than happy to allow her to marry into the de Lisle family, since the Laceys, although once wealthy, had come down in the world, and Selina brought almost nothing with her.'

'Oh?' said Angela. 'Did the de Lisles approve of the arrangement? I thought you said they liked to use marriage as a way to increase their fortunes, rather than admit people to the family who could not benefit them.'

'They were indeed,' agreed Mr. Gilverson. 'Roger, especially, was strongly in favour of that sort of method of attaining wealth, since it had worked very well for his family in the past—although he also had a deep attachment to the de Lisle name, and was proud of his antecedents, and was especially keen for the blood-line to remain pure and unsullied by inter-marriage with those of less glorious lineage. And yet he very much supported the marriage—encouraged it, even. Perhaps he had decided to move with the times—who can tell? At any rate, Edgar and Selina were married after a very short engagement, and she moved to Greystone Chase to live with the de Lisles while he went back to France.

'Now, the de Lisles were a very particular sort of family, and it takes a particular sort of person to rub along with them. I first met Selina shortly after the wedding, and I remember feeling a certain sense of foreboding at the time. She was very young—not more than eighteen—and very pretty, as one might expect. She was tremendously gay and lively, and appeared full of genuine good humour, but when she thought nobody was looking I occasionally glimpsed a sideways look in her eye which gave me the strongest impression that here was someone who liked to make mischief.'

'Oh? In what way?' said Angela, interested despite herself.

'Well, for one thing, she had a way of making a remark which *seemed* innocent enough on the surface, but which was evidently directed at someone in particular, for one would sense a sudden stiffening in the atmosphere, and the subject would turn. Then perhaps later on another member of the family would fail to appear at luncheon, and Selina would say that she was very much afraid she might have unwittingly offended someone by something she had said earlier. Then she would laugh, and say she would never understand the funny old ways of the family, but that she would make it up to the person later. And she was bold, too. She took liberties that would not have been allowed from anyone else in the family, and got away with them simply because she was daring enough to try them. From my observations, I had the feeling that she was a girl who was very easily bored and constantly in search of entertainment—which was understandable enough, since the de Lisles lived a quiet life.

'Selina's brother Henry was also staying at Greystone while I was there. I understand he had taken advantage of his sister's marriage to impose upon the de Lisles' hospitality as frequently as possible. I didn't take to the fellow myself, and I gather the feeling was shared by most of the family. There was something underhanded about him. It wasn't something one could put one's finger on, but he always seemed to be sneaking about the house. I never caught him at it, but I shouldn't have been surprised if he'd been the sort to listen at doors.'

'Dear me,' said Angela, who was not above listening at doors herself in the pursuit of justice, although of course that was quite a different thing.

'So, Selina remained at Greystone Chase while her husband was away,' went on Mr. Gilverson, 'although of course he spent all his leave there with her. When he was not there things carried on as they had done before. Godfrey de Lisle married and brought his wife, Victorine, to live at Greystone Chase, but other than that little of note happened.'

'Victorine? She was French, I take it,' said Angela.

'Yes. Godfrey had known her since they were children. She was a little older than he and was as unlike Selina as possible. One doesn't wish to be unchivalrous but I am afraid she was rather plain, and her looks were not assisted by her manner, which was dour to say the least. Evelyn and she took a great liking to one another, however—perhaps united by their dislike of Selina.'

'Evelyn disliked her son's wife? I thought you said the de Lisles approved of the marriage.'

'Ah, yes,' said Mr. Gilverson. 'There I may have misled you slightly. When I refer to the de Lisles, for the most part I mean Roger de Lisle. In reality nobody else mattered. Roger was the head of the family in the most traditional sense. He ruled ruthlessly and absolutely. If he issued a decree then there was no gainsaying it. He would have his way and nobody could dissuade him without feeling his temper.'

'I see,' said Angela. 'Then Edgar—Mr. de Lisle—could not have married Selina without his father's permission.'

'I shouldn't say that exactly,' said Mr. Gilverson. 'Edgar was of age, after all. However, he knew his father, and knew that if he went against Roger's wishes then either he or his mother would suffer for it—most likely his mother, for Edgar might go where he pleased, of course, while Evelyn had no choice but to stay at home.'

'Did nobody ever go against Roger's wishes, then?'

'Not as a general rule. There was some dispute between Edgar and his father over Edgar's wish to go into the blood-stock business instead of the family wine-making concern, but I don't know how it ended. As far as I know it was still unresolved when my nephew was arrested for his wife's murder.'

Angela was silent for a second, remembering what Valencourt had said that day in Hyde Park. He was planning to go to South America to breed horses, he said. It was what he had always meant to do.

'Tell me about the murder,' she said. 'Why did they think Mr. de Lisle had done it?'

Mr. Gilverson hesitated. He seemed to be looking for the right words.

'The marriage was a mistake, I think,' he said at last. 'They fell in love too quickly, and just as quickly the thing burnt itself out. They were two of a kind, he and she—both attractive, lively, charming people—but in the end they were too similar, and it led to conflict. Edgar was away much of the time and Selina was bored. She craved excitement, but there was none to be had at Greystone, and she blamed him for it. I don't doubt she loved him, but I believe part of the reason she married him was to have the freedom she could not have had as an unmarried orphan girl. And there was no freedom at Greystone. Everyone bowed to the will of Roger de Lisle. All that was left for her to do was to create discord among the family. It is a great pity,' he finished. 'I didn't especially like

Selina, but I don't believe she was a bad person. She certainly did not deserve to die the way she did.'

'How did she die?' said Angela, although she did not want to know the answer.

'She was strangled,' said Gilverson. 'Her body was found in a little wood in the grounds of Greystone Chase. She had been expecting a child and it died with her.'

Angela looked down at the floor. It was worse than she had feared.

'Yes,' said Mr. Gilverson. 'It was very unpleasant. Such a violent end for such a young girl. And I'm afraid all the evidence pointed to Edgar's having done it.'

Angela wanted to ask something but could not. Mr. Gilverson saw her questioning gaze and went on:

'I shall tell you all the facts as I know them, since I was not there at the time. It all happened one Sunday in late April. Edgar was home on leave and was due to return to duty in the next day or two. At some time in the afternoon he and Selina were overheard by Godfrey and Victorine de Lisle engaged in a quarrel, after which Selina declared she was feeling unwell and went up to her room to lie down.'

'What was the quarrel about?'

'The witnesses could not say. My nephew later testified that it was nothing of any moment, and that he shortly afterwards followed her upstairs and begged her pardon, after which all was well again between them. According to Evelyn de Lisle's maid, who had been sent to attend to her, Selina spent most of the afternoon in bed. She was certainly not seen downstairs again. Some time in the early evening, a servant came to report that Selina was still indisposed and intended to spend the rest of the evening in her room, and that she did not want dinner or to be disturbed. According to Edgar, he knocked on her door as he went up to dress, but there was no reply so he assumed she was asleep. He knocked again later that evening as he went up to bed, but again received no reply. He tried the door but found it locked, and so gave it up and thought nothing more of it.

'The next morning, it was discovered that the door was now unlocked and that Selina had gone missing. At first it was thought that she had gone out early for a walk in the grounds, although she was not in the habit of doing so, but when lunch-time came and she still had not turned up a search was begun. She was found a little time later. It was Edgar himself who found her. He raised the alarm immediately, but it was too late, for she had evidently been dead for some time.

'The police were called, of course, and at first they believed—as did everybody—that Selina had taken herself out for a walk early that morning, for some reason best known to herself, and that she had been attacked by an unknown assailant. But this was swiftly disproved by the medical evidence, which indicated that she had not died that morning at all, but the day before. Of course, that fact directed their attention towards the members of the household, since as far as anybody knew, Selina had spent the whole of the previous day in the house—and natu-rally, the first person to come under suspicion in cases such as these is the husband. Unfortunately, the very fact of Edgar's having found her looked suspicious, since her body had been half-concealed in some undergrowth and was not easy to see. His story was that his eye had been caught by a glimpse of her dress, which was of a vivid pink, but the police jumped to a different conclusion, and assumed that the reason he had known where to find her was because he had killed her. It wasn't long before the police found out about the row of the day before, and after that their investigations tended in only one direction. It was clear they believed that the dispute had continued later and that Edgar had killed Selina in a fit of anger.'

'But his finding the body is surely not in itself enough to suggest that he did it,' said Angela.

'No,' said Mr. Gilverson, 'but other facts soon came to light which made things look very black for him. The police began a search of the house, and it was not long before they found clear evidence that Selina had been killed indoors—or at least hidden indoors for some time after her death.'

'Oh?' said Angela.

'Yes,' said Mr. Gilverson. He hesitated, and then went on, 'In Edgar's room was a large cupboard which was rarely or never used. Inside that the police found a hair-comb which was identified as Selina's, with one or two long, fair hairs still attached to it. They also found a tiny scrap of pink fabric caught on a loose nail, which was later shown to have come from Selina's dress. There was no reason at all for those things to have been in the cupboard unless Selina had gone in there herself, and why should she have done that when she was alive? Furthermore, the inside of the cupboard was very dusty, but the dust had clearly been disturbed by a heavy object of some sort. When they came to examine the body, they found streaks of dust on her dress in addition to the scraps of vegetation from the bed of leaves on which she had been found. It all pointed to Edgar's having killed Selina in the house and hidden her body in the cupboard until everybody had gone to bed, after which he took her outside and disposed of her in the wood. It was thought that he had also locked her bedroom door so that nobody would go in and discover she was missing before he had had a chance to get rid of the body. Of course, it all looked conclusive enough. The police certainly thought so, and arrested him. You know the rest.'

'I see,' said Angela. At that moment she wanted more than anything to leave the place immediately and refuse to hear any more. The urge was so overwhelming that she made to rise, and would certainly have been out of the room the next second, but before she could act on her impulse she happened to catch sight of Mr. Gilverson's face as a shadow passed fleetingly across it. He had kept his sorrow well hidden up to now, but that one look was enough to convince her that he had been deeply affected by it all. Here, at least, was someone who did not believe in his nephew's guilt—or at least, did not *want* to believe in it. Instead of standing up, therefore, she hesitated, and said:

'You say he didn't do it. Why do you think that?'

'Because Edgar was not a violent man. It was completely out of character for him to do such a thing.'

'But the evidence—'

'Yes, yes, there was no denying the evidence,' he said. 'And yet I believed in his innocence. I still do.'

'Was there nothing you could do then?'

'Very little,' said Gilverson. 'You see, Roger and I had fallen out a few weeks earlier—or shall we say I was in his bad books, and was not welcome at Greystone. The news of Edgar's arrest did not reach me as soon as it might have. Naturally I did what I could in the way of legal assistance, but by then the story had got out and people were already saying he had done it, and the rest of the family were maintaining what I should call a loud silence, which said as clearly as anything that they thought him guilty. Then there was the trial, which was over shamefully quickly and could have only one verdict under the circumstances, and after that there was nothing to be done.'

'Didn't his family have anything to say in his defence?' said Angela.

'Very little,' said Gilverson. 'In fact, his own brother testified to having overheard the row between the two of them. Naturally he could not lie in court if he *had* overheard it, but I've always wondered why he felt the need to mention it at all.'

'And what about Roger and Evelyn de Lisle? Did they give evidence in court?'

'I believe they did, but only as it related to the movements of everybody in the house on the day Selina died. Nothing quite as damning as the evidence of the quarrel.'

Angela pondered for a moment, then said:

'Very well, then, if Mr. de Lisle didn't kill his wife, who did? I don't suppose it's possible that someone from outside the house might have come in and done it?'

'It's highly unlikely,' said Mr. Gilverson. 'Naturally, inquiries were instituted in the area, but no-one reported having seen anything unusual or suspicious.'

'Then presumably the murderer was someone in the house.'

'Presumably, yes,' said Mr. Gilverson.

'But who?' said Angela. 'Who was in the house on the day of the murder?'

'The family, of course: Roger and Evelyn; Godfrey and Victorine; Edgar, naturally. Henry Lacey was also staying there at the time, as was an old school-friend of his called Oliver Harrington, who was on leave and had come to visit for a day or two. I don't know what became of him.'

'And none of them came under suspicion at the time?'

'Seemingly not. The police had a perfectly good suspect in front of their noses, and why should they look any more deeply into it?'

Angela fell silent, for exactly the same thing might have been said about her own arrest and trial. The case against her had seemed water-tight at the time, and yet she had been innocent. Might the same be true of Edgar Valencourt? It was an uncomfortable thought, but that, after all, was why she was here. Despite the unusual circumstances (to say the least) and her vow never to involve herself in another murder inquiry, her interest was aroused by the story Mr. Gilverson had told. There were one or two points which did not seem to fit what she had herself known of Valencourt. Despite his dubious choice of career, she had known him to be a generally good-tempered, rational, intelligent man who thought before he acted, and was certainly not prone to being thrown into a panic or acting rashly. If he really had murdered his wife, then why had he hidden her body in his room? Since he had supposedly locked *her* door to make it look as though she were in bed and did not

THE SHADOW AT GREYSTONE CHASE

wish to be disturbed, surely it would have made more sense to put her (or leave her, depending on where she had been killed) in her own room, so as not to leave any traces in his. And if he were guilty, then why had he made sure that he was the one to find her body, when he must have known it would have drawn attention upon him? None of this seemed to add up to the man she had known. That was not to say he was innocent, of course, but it certainly looked as though the matter bore further investigation. She had answered the summons unwillingly, but by turning up here at all she had as good as agreed to do it. However, there were some practical difficulties to be got over first, which would require a certain degree of openness between her and the solicitor. Reluctantly, she decided to lay some of her cards upon the table.

'Mr. Gilverson,' she said at last, 'I'm sure I don't need to tell you that I'd much rather not be here now. The only reason I came is because—for various reasons—I feel bound by honour to carry out Mr. de Lisle's wishes. I will do as he asks, as I expect he knew I would, although in truth, even if he is innocent I don't see how I can find out anything that the police did not discover at the time—especially not after so many years. Still, I'll do what I can. However, you must be aware that I cannot simply sweep in and start asking questions of everyone. People will certainly wonder why I am attempting to help clear the name of the man who is supposed to have killed my husband.'

She stopped uncomfortably, thinking she had perhaps said too much. Mr. Gilverson held up his hand.

'Please do not upset yourself,' he said. 'I said there was no need to refer to the subject and I meant it. Of course you are right, and if you will believe me, I tried very hard to dissuade my nephew from writing to you at all. There is no helping him now, and I certainly have no wish to see you get into a scrape on his behalf.'

'A scrape,' repeated Angela, half-amused. 'You might call it that, I suppose.'

Mr. Gilverson smiled.

'You say you consider yourself honour-bound to do this,' he said, 'but believe me, you are quite at liberty to change your mind now if you like. Nobody will think the worse of you—I shall not, at any rate, and Edgar is no longer here to care about it one way or the other. Still, if you do decide to do it, I have been thinking that the only way to go about it will be for you to go in disguise.'

'In disguise!' exclaimed Angela. 'What, do you mean in a wig and a false moustache?'

'No, no, nothing so extreme,' said Mr. Gilverson, laughing. 'Perhaps disguise was the wrong word. Shall we say incognito instead? A false name.'

'Oh, I see,' said Angela. 'Yes, of course, that would be the only way. But even then I still can't simply turn up and begin asking questions of complete strangers. Do the family still live at Greystone Chase?'

'Godfrey and Victorine de Lisle spend part of the year there, but not the others,' said Mr. Gilverson.

'Oh? Did they return to France?'

'No. Evelyn de Lisle died shortly after Edgar's trial—some said of a broken heart, since Edgar was her favourite son, although I think that is fanciful, myself. Roger died some three years ago. I propose you commence your investigations by speaking to Godfrey and Victorine.'

'But how?'

Mr. Gilverson smiled.

'Nothing easier,' he said. 'Greystone Chase is at present up for sale. I shall write you a letter of introduction and tell them you are interested in buying the place. I shall tell them some cock and bull story about how I know you, and that will get you their acquaintance.'

'Oh!' said Angela, thinking. 'Yes, that is a plan, certainly. I wonder, though: will a visit or two to the house be enough to find out what I want to know? It seems to me it would be better if I went down there and scouted about a bit first. Where is Greystone Chase, exactly? Perhaps there are people still living nearby who remember what happened and can tell me more.'

'I dare say there are,' said Mr. Gilverson. 'Greystone is situated on the outskirts of Denborough, so perhaps you might begin your inquiries there, as the family are very well known in the area. Do you know Denborough at all? It's a small seaside resort which is popular with elderly and retired gentlefolk, although at this time of year I expect it will be fairly quiet.'

'Elderly and retired gentlefolk?' said Angela. 'Then I had better pack my flannel petticoats and most comfortable shoes. One doesn't wish to stand out.'

'No indeed,' said Mr. Gilverson, with an amused look. 'Then you have definitely decided to do it?'

'I suppose so,' said Angela resignedly.

Mr. Gilverson seemed pleased.

'But I can't promise anything,' she went on quickly. 'It was all such a long time ago that people are bound to have forgotten things. Are you quite sure you've told me everything you know?'

'Not everything,' said Mr. Gilverson. 'I should like you to approach the case with an open mind and make your own deductions, and if I told you all I know I should inevitably put my own interpretation on the facts, which is hardly conducive to your reaching a fair conclusion. Go to Denborough and speak to the people there. You will bring a new pair of eyes and ears to the case, and perhaps will find out something that was missed eleven years ago.'

'Well, I shall try,' said Angela.

So it was agreed, and Angela rose to take her leave, promising to keep the solicitor apprised of developments. After she had gone, Gilverson sat for a few moments, as though considering what had just passed.

'Skittish,' he said to himself at last. 'Understandable, of course. She doesn't want to do it, and I expect she'll be frightened off easily. Still, it's worth a try. Who knows whether she mightn't come up with something useful?'

CHAPTER FIVE

THE REGENT HOTEL in Denborough was a grand relic of former glories. Fifty years earlier the little town had been a thriving holiday resort, welcoming the fashionable end of London society as well as the more discerning members of the affluent middle classes. Times change, however, and in recent years the *haut monde* had moved on to Juan-les-Pins and the Riviera, while those in the lower tier had discovered that Devon was both prettier and warmer. These days, therefore, the Regent attracted mainly elderly people who had come to the place every year in their youth and saw no reason to change their habits now.

'It is so pleasant to see a new face here,' said Mrs. Hudd, inclining her head graciously towards the new guest by whom she was seated. 'The Regent is a delightful hotel, but I fear one tends to see the same people year after year. Shall you be staying here long, Mrs. Wells?'

'I don't know yet,' replied Angela. 'This place was recommended to me quite by chance, but I must say it is very pretty. The sea air is very bracing, too.'

'Indeed it is,' said Miss Atkinson, who sat to Mrs. Hudd's other side. 'I know some people call it chilly, but I always think too much warm weather can be quite stifling, and heat isn't at all good for the lungs, you know. I don't understand why anyone would prefer to go abroad when we have everything we need here at home.'

'Oh, quite,' said Angela, who was wearing two layers of clothing more than she liked for the time of year, and who would have been quite happy to sacrifice her lungs in exchange for some warm sunshine.

They were sitting in the elegant lounge of the hotel, the most stately of the grand buildings in a faded Crescent which some enterprising local business-man had built on the sea front in the early years of the town's prosperity. The Crescent was situated in the finest part of Denborough, and the Regent was in the finest part of the Crescent—at the very centre, which gave it a direct and unobstructed view of Denborough Bay. Other, lesser hotels, nearer the outer edges of the Crescent, had inferior views and a correspondingly inferior clientele. Angela had arrived at the Regent the day before and had been swiftly pounced upon by Mrs. Hudd (Mrs. Beatrice Hudd of the Staffordshire Hudds, as she hastened to mention—*not* the ironmongery people, oh dear, no!) and Miss Atkinson, who lived in Surrey but had been a Kentish girl. The two ladies came at the same time every year and feasted upon such social glory as remained in the town these days. The arrival of Mrs. Wells was a cause of great excitement to them both, and was tempered by only a little initial reserve at the newcomer's relative youth and high social standing, as evidenced by the fact that she brought with her a lady's maid. Angela's easy manner and lack of self-importance soon dissipated any doubts they may have had, however, and in less than twenty-four hours she had been welcomed into their little circle and was fast becoming privy to their thoughts on everybody and everything.

'If you are not familiar with the area, let me assure you that there are many beauties hereabouts,' said Mrs. Hudd. 'Besides the bay itself, I mean. Fallow Hill, for example, is a noted landmark which you would be wise not to miss. There are also a number of country parks, although some of the finest ones are private and not open to visitors.'

'Oh, yes,' said Miss Atkinson. 'Brancome Hall is simply delightful. I visit it every year and it never disappoints.'

'Brancome Hall? Is that the large house one passes shortly before turning onto the Denborough road?' said Angela, although she knew very well that it was not.

'No, Brancome is quite in the other direction—farther along the coast towards Ramsgate,' said Mrs. Hudd. 'I believe the house to which you are referring is Greystone Chase.' She drew herself up disapprovingly. 'A very odd place. It belongs to the French.'

'What, all of them?' said Angela.

Miss Atkinson tittered behind her hand.

'Not exactly,' she said. 'Mrs. Hudd means they are a family from France.'

'I am not fond of the French,' said Mrs. Hudd. 'They cheated the late Mr. Hudd in the matter of a painting many years ago. He was given quite unequivocally to understand that it was by one of the Masters, but it turned out to be a forgery—although they *called* it a copy. Five pounds is not a sum to throw away lightly. The experience distressed him greatly, and he was still talking of it during his final illness.'

'Goodness,' said Angela.

'At any rate,' went on Mrs. Hudd, 'Greystone Chase is a private house and not open to the public.'

'There were some terrible goings-on there a few years ago,' said Miss Atkinson. 'It was quite a scandal, and I don't believe they ever got over it.'

'Oh? What happened?' said Angela.

Miss Atkinson adopted a suitably solemn expression.

'I'm afraid it was all quite dreadful,' she said. 'One of the sons of the house killed his young wife.'

'Dear me!' said Angela.

'Foreigners,' said Mrs. Hudd, with a shake of the head.

'He was caught, of course,' said Miss Atkinson. 'Such a disgrace for the rest of the family to have to live down.'

Angela was about to question Miss Atkinson further, when Mrs. Hudd sat up and said:

'Oh, it is Colonel Dempster! Good afternoon, colonel!'

The newcomer to whom she referred was a gentleman of stiff moustache and upright bearing, who had evidently expanded outwards in recent years, for it appeared that some violence had been employed to force the buttons of his tweed suit through the button-holes. He was still a fine man, however, and it quickly became clear that he had at least two female admirers in the shape of Mrs. Hudd and Miss Atkinson, for the former seemed to soften a little in his presence, while the latter sat up and somehow became less self-effacing. Colonel Dempster was introduced to Mrs. Wells, who declared herself charmed with the area. At that, the colonel puffed up in satisfaction, putting an alarming strain on his middle button. He was a local man himself, he said—lived just a short distance away in a modest little cottage close to the sea—quite enough for him and Betsy (here he indicated a black spaniel which had flopped at his feet when he sat down)—was always happy to see his friends Mrs. Hudd and Miss Atkinson—and how long was Mrs. Wells thinking of staying?

Angela said what was proper, but was a little vexed that the colonel had arrived just as she had been about to find out something about the subject of most interest to her. She was wondering how to turn the conversation back in that direction, when Miss Atkinson said, most conveniently:

'We have just been telling Mrs. Wells about the dreadful events at Greystone Chase, colonel. I believe you knew the family.'

Colonel Dempster coughed and gave something that might have been a little shudder.

'I did indeed,' he said. 'Terrible thing, it was. Terrible. Never thought I should see such wickedness in a fellow officer. Never should have thought it of him. A bad apple, he was. A very bad apple.'

He shook his head and subsided into silence.

'I was telling you of Miss Lacey,' said Miss Atkinson. 'She was a local girl who married the younger son of the family. I am very much afraid to say that he killed her in a fit of rage.'

'The blackguard strangled her!' roared the colonel suddenly. 'No way to treat a woman. He brought shame upon his family.'

'What can one expect of the French?' said Mrs. Hudd, who had no personal connection with the matter but did not intend to let that prevent her from pronouncing judgment.

'They weren't wholly French,' said the colonel. Mrs. de Lisle was an Englishwoman through and through. I knew her when she was a girl. I called her Evelyn and she called me Bertie. Delightful woman, delightful. She died of a broken heart after it all happened.'

Miss Atkinson nodded soberly.

'I am afraid she did,' she said. 'Of course, they didn't call it that, but it all comes down to the same thing in the end.'

'Will you have tea, colonel?' said Mrs. Hudd, who liked to return the attention of the company to herself at regular intervals.

There was some little bustle as tea was arranged, then Angela returned to the original subject.

'I seem to remember hearing something about the case, once,' she said. 'Wasn't there some doubt as to the guilt of Mr. de Lisle?'

'None at all, as far as I know,' said the colonel. 'He killed her and then shoved her body in a cupboard as though it were a pair of old shoes. The evidence was quite clear. They found the fellow guilty, but he escaped and went on the run for years, and only reappeared a few months ago when it turned out he'd killed someone else too. You probably read about it in the newspapers.'

'I think I did,' said Angela vaguely.

'So you see, he was most definitely the murderous sort,' said the colonel. 'There's no doubt he did it. He's dead now, of course.'

'I suppose the family must have left Greystone Chase after it all happened,' said Angela.

'No,' said Mrs. Hudd, thankful for an opportunity to take part in the conversation once again. 'They are still here. One sees Mrs. de Lisle in particular out and about in the town.'

'Another Mrs. de Lisle?' said Angela. 'How many are there?'

'Only one,' said the colonel. 'Wife of the eldest son, Godfrey. There's only the two of them left. He and she.'

'Now, she is most definitely French,' said Mrs. Hudd. 'We have exchanged greetings and she has a quite pronounced accent.'

'Yes, she is,' conceded the colonel. 'A good lady, by all accounts.'

He spoke of her with some reserve. It occurred to Angela that he did not admire Victorine de Lisle, and she remembered what Mr. Gilverson had said about her being plain. The conversation had now turned to other matters and Angela took the opportunity to reflect on her good fortune. She had come to Denborough with the intention of picking up local gossip without looking too suspicious, and had thought that a hotel might be a good place to start, but she had never dreamed that she would be so successful so soon. To have been introduced to Colonel Dempster, who had actually known the de Lisles personally at the time of the murder, was a stroke of luck indeed. It seemed almost too much of a coincidence, but Angela supposed that in a small place such as Denborough it was only to be expected that many of the residents knew or had known the de Lisles. She resolved to make the colonel's closer acquaintance if she could. Perhaps he could give her more information than she had had so far, for at present there was nothing at all to suggest that a mistake had been made, or that Edgar Valencourt had not murdered his wife.

CHAPTER SIX

THE NEXT MORNING dawned fine, although to judge from the movement of the grass on the cliff top, there was still a brisk breeze blowing. Angela looked out of her bedroom window and gave a little shiver.

'Blessed are we who bring with us warm underthings,' she remarked to Marthe.

'I do not understand why anyone should want to go to the English seaside at this time of year,' said Marthe, who was tidying up the dressing-table. 'Why do all these elderly ladies insist on coming here to take walks in the freezing cold in the morning and in the afternoon and in the evening? And then they complain about the stiffness in their bones and seem surprised that they can no longer bend down. It makes no sense. Me, I think they are mad. It is much pleasanter and warmer on the Continent.'

'I dare say it is,' said Angela. 'But then they would have to speak to the natives and eat the food, and that might kill them. Or at the very least scare them into fits.'

'It would be pleasanter for you too, *madame*,' said Marthe, who did not approve of this latest adventure. 'You should not be here.'

'Perhaps not,' said Angela, 'but I promised I'd do it, so onward I must go.'

'But what kind of person would hold you to your word?' said Marthe. 'This solicitor ought not to have written to you in the first place. It was an inelegant thing to do.'

'Inelegant?' said Angela, amused.

'Yes,' said Marthe. 'It is not kind to put a lady in such a position, and nobody will think the worse of you if you change your mind. Write to him and tell him you no longer wish to do it. You will never hear from him again, and you can leave this place and forget everything.'

Since Angela had been trying for months to forget everything with little success, this was hardly useful advice. She made no comment, however, but merely said:

'I gave my word and I mean to keep it. I dare say I won't find anything out, but nobody will be able to say that I didn't try.'

Marthe saw that her mistress's mind was made up, and shook her head sadly.

'It pains me to see you so restless, *madame*,' she said. 'You travel here and you travel there, and never do you stop.'

'I like it,' said Angela. 'One gets terribly bored staying in the same place all the time.'

As a matter of fact, she had begun to toy with the idea of returning to America within the next few months. During her time in England she had neglected her business rather, and although she trusted absolutely the man she had left in charge, she felt that she had been gone too long and had forgotten too much. Now she had received a letter from someone who had expressed an interest in buying the company, and the thought tempted her more than she had expected. After so many years of hard work it would be pleasant to hand everything over to someone else, she thought. She could return to the States and negotiate the thing personally. Perhaps she would even stay a while. There she would be anonymous once more—no longer the notorious Mrs. Marchmont who had been tried for murder, but plain old Mrs. Marchmont who could walk down the street without feeling that everybody was staring and whispering as she passed. America had been her home for fifteen years and lately she had found herself missing the place—its free-and-easiness; its lack of pretence; the belief, shared by all, that anyone might be successful if only they worked hard enough. Such a contrast to the formality and stuffiness of England, where family and connections counted for everything. Of course, now there was Barbara to consider she could not simply move back without a second thought, but perhaps Barbara would like to come with her. There were many excellent colleges there, and perhaps the place would be more suited to her daughter's temperament and independent nature. Still, that was a matter for the future. For now she had other things to think about and a murder to investigate.

'I think I had better put on a warm scarf,' she said to Marthe. 'The green one will do.'

'What are you going to do this morning?' said Marthe.

'I am going to attempt to charm an elderly gentleman,' said Angela. 'If I can find him, that is.'

Putting on her scarf and hat, she left her room and went down in the rickety old lift to the hotel lobby. From there she emerged onto the Crescent, which overlooked a large patch of green on the cliff top. One or two people were walking their dogs there, but Colonel Dempster was not among them, so Angela set forth towards the edge of the cliff, where a steep flight of steps descended onto the beach. She paused at the top and looked about her. The place was certainly very fine when the sun was shining and the wind had dropped, although the stubbornly stiff breeze and the large clouds that blew frequently across the sun prevented the day from being really warm.

'Morning,' said a voice beside her, and Angela looked round to see a woman of late middle age who had stopped likewise to admire the view from the top of the cliff. She was pushing a wheel-chair in which sat another woman, as far as Angela could judge from the number of scarves, shawls and blankets that enveloped her.

'Good morning,' replied Angela politely.

'That do you, Jemmy?' said the woman, bending over the chair.

The patient uttered a sound which might have indicated assent, and lifted a hand weakly to point at something. Her other hand lay useless in her lap.

'No, I don't think that's the same boat as yesterday,' said her companion. 'The other one had a red stripe and a white sail, don't you remember? This one here's got a brown sail.'

The woman in the wheel-chair gave what looked like a nod of the head, and slumped further down into her seat.

'A fit to the brain,' explained the first woman to Angela. 'A stroke, they called it.'

'Is she your patient?' said Angela.

The woman shook her head.

'My sister,' she said. 'Took ill a month ago, she did. The doctors shake their heads but she's not ready to go yet.'

'And are you nursing her? That must be hard work.'

'Not me,' said the woman cheerfully. 'She's in one of these fancy nursing-homes. Ever so nice, it is. I joke to them that when she's gone I wouldn't mind her bed.'

She seemed unduly good-humoured for someone whose sister was so gravely ill, and must have realized this, for she went on:

'Don't think me unfeeling, dear. Jemmy's had a good life, all things considered. She was always a simple one—sickly too, as a child. She's done well to get to the age she has. When she fell sick she wanted to come back here to Denborough, where she was brought up, so I thought to myself, why not? She'd been away long enough. They're all dead now, and this used to be her home, after all. She's being well cared for where she is, and I visit her, and take her out, and she's as happy as she can be.'

Here the patient shifted and coughed at something, and they looked up to see a rather striking-looking woman passing, a little dog sniffing at her heels. She was perhaps a little older than Angela, and dressed soberly in the English manner, but there was a smartness about her, and something slightly exotic that did not quite fit the place. She smiled pleasantly at the little group as she passed. Jemmy made a sound, and her sister said:

'Very well, then, we'll go that way. Not too far, mind, or I'll have to push you a long way uphill on the way back.'

She turned the chair with some difficulty and, with a friendly salute to Angela, continued on her way along the cliff path. Angela watched her go, then descended the steps onto the beach. Down below the cliffs gave some shelter from the wind, and Angela felt warm enough to remove her scarf. She had no idea at what time the colonel walked his dog, but he had the weather-beaten appearance of a man who spent much of his time in the open air, and so she expected he would be found frequently out and about. From her brief encounter with him the day before she judged him to be the sort who liked the company of ladies, and she hoped he would be amenable to making the acquaintance of another. She wanted to talk to him and learn more about the de Lisles. In particular she wanted to know why, if the family had not cared whether their younger son were found guilty of murder or not, Evelyn de Lisle should have died of a broken heart shortly afterwards. The two facts did not seem to fit.

Angela walked along the beach a little way, but could not see the colonel anywhere. After a few hundred yards she spied a little cottage that was not quite on the beach, which she thought might belong to him, and stopped outside it. It was neat and trim, with a yellow-painted door, and under the doorbell was a plate that said 'Dempster.' Angela pressed the bell, but no-one answered—rather to her relief, since she had realized somewhat belatedly that she could think of no excuse for calling. She returned along the beach and ascended the steps. At the top she saw Mrs. Hudd, who had evidently just left the hotel, walking towards her without her acolyte Miss Atkinson. Mrs. Hudd greeted her graciously.

'Good morning,' said Angela. 'Where is your friend today?'

'Miss Atkinson unfortunately has a blister,' replied Mrs. Hudd. 'She walked too far the other day and practically tore the skin off her right foot, but did not help herself by continuing to walk on it yesterday when she ought to have rested it. We fear it may have gone septic, and so she is staying indoors today and keeping her foot up on my advice. She would have bandaged it up and come out if I had allowed her to.' She lowered her voice. 'To be perfectly truthful, Mrs. Wells, I sometimes have my doubts about her common sense, and wonder how she spent so many years in the teaching profession. But then she does play the piano rather sweetly, so I suppose that must count for something.'

'I suppose it must,' said Angela politely. 'Then you are alone today.'

'Yes,' said Mrs. Hudd. 'Perhaps you would like to take a walk with me?'

'I should be glad to,' said Angela. Mrs. Hudd was not precisely the person she wanted to speak to, but she was obviously a gossip and so Angela hoped she might find out something useful.

They walked along the cliff top in the opposite direction to the one Angela had taken in her walk along the beach.

'You have been coming here for years, I gather,' said Angela.

'Oh, yes,' said Mrs. Hudd. 'The late Mr. Hudd and I came here when we first married and the place has associations for me now. I do believe I could never go anywhere else. The air is so healthy, don't you think?'

Angela, snug once more in her scarf, spoke with animation of the sharpness of the air, and the two ladies continued on their way. The cliff top now began to slope downwards gradually, until it finally disappeared and the path became a promenade. Here there was another stretch of sand which was invisible from the other beach, and the first thing Angela saw on it was an erect and portly figure coming towards them, accompanied by a black spaniel with a stick in its mouth. She suppressed a sigh of irritation, for now she was with Mrs. Hudd and would not be able to bring up the subject about which she wanted to speak to him.

Mrs. Hudd had seen the colonel too, and raised her voice to greet him. He bowed gallantly to them, and Mrs. Hudd preened girlishly. The two of them conversed enthusiastically about the glories of the day as Angela looked on.

'I've just been speaking to Mrs. Poynter,' said the colonel, once the topic of the weather had been exhausted to their satisfaction. 'She's got rats.'

'Dear me!' said Mrs. Hudd, putting her hand to her breast in alarm.

'Yes,' said the colonel, nodding. 'Her husband is away in Birmingham until next week, and she says she keeps hearing scrabbling sounds in the attic. That little terrier of hers is scared of its own shadow, so that's no help. Betsy's no good as a ratter either, poor old thing,' he went on, bending down to pat his dog's head affectionately, 'or I'd offer her services. I expect it will have to be poison.'

'Isn't she afraid, all alone in the house with the rats?' said Mrs. Hudd.

'No, no, not she,' said the colonel. 'She's not the nam-by-pamby sort. She's made of stern stuff despite her looks.'

'Oh, her looks,' said Mrs. Hudd carelessly. 'I don't admire the type myself, but I can see why some might call her attractive.'

Angela had no idea who Mrs. Poynter was, but evidently she was not a favourite of Mrs. Hudd.

'Shall we turn back, Mrs. Wells, and walk with the colonel?' said that lady now, and did so without waiting for Angela's reply.

They returned along the beach as far as the cliff steps and ascended them once more, then Colonel Dempster escorted them back to the hotel, where luncheon was just being served, and took his leave. Angela and Mrs. Hudd were then joined by Miss Atkinson, who was evidently chafing under her enforced inactivity, and Mrs. Hudd spent most of lunch in lecturing her friend, who took it meekly and agreed to remain sitting for the rest of the afternoon, at least. Meanwhile, Angela amused herself by observing the relationship between the two. Mrs.

Hudd seemed to be the one in charge—at least, she certainly thought so—but Angela thought she could discern a little gleam of rebellion in Miss Atkinson's eye, which told her that here was someone who was not so easily cowed as it might appear.

After lunch, Angela found that a letter had arrived for her. It was from Mr. Gilverson, who informed her that Mr. and Mrs. de Lisle were only too delighted to invite Mrs. Wells to come and see Greystone Chase. Business would prevent Mr. de Lisle from conducting Mrs. Wells around the place himself, but he assured her that she would be given every attention and had only to ask if there were anything she wished to know.

'I don't know why Godfrey can't show you around in person,' finished the letter. 'Pure laziness on his part, I expect. It's all rather inconvenient, of course, since the whole point of the thing was to get you an introduction to him. Still, you might at least get a sight of him or Victorine, who is a little shy and awkward but, I hope, not so much so as deliberately to avoid someone who has come with a view to purchasing her house.'

Angela had mixed feelings on reading the letter. She had spent two days in Denborough, at best skirting around the edges of the matter, but now was the time when she must go into the lion's den itself. She was nervous at the thought of visiting Edgar Valencourt's family home, although she could not quite say why. She quashed the feeling, however, and set her jaw. She had made the promise, and must carry it through. She would go to Greystone Chase and find out what she could, then report back to Mr. Gilverson. If she discovered nothing then that was as far as her investigation was likely to take her,

for she could hardly prowl about the place with a magnify-
ing-glass, looking for evidence that probably did not exist. A
little voice whispered in her ear that she did not *want* to find
evidence, but she ignored it, for that line of thought led down
a path she did not wish to follow.

CHAPTER SEVEN

THE NEXT DAY Miss Atkinson's foot was much better, and she and Mrs. Hudd decided to take a trip to Canterbury, on which Angela was invited to join them. She agreed, partly for something to do, and partly because she was keen to spend a few hours away from the chill of the seaside. The little party spent a pleasant morning touring the city, and Angela was duly impressed by the Cathedral and its bloody history. After lunch, they spent a little time wandering through the cobbled streets, and returned to the hotel in time for an early tea. The napkins were just being laid out when Mrs. Hudd looked up and said:

'Who is that person?'

Angela glanced around to see whom she was talking about, and her eyes widened in surprise as she saw a young man standing in the doorway of the dining-room, looking about him as though seeking somebody. He had the air of someone supremely at ease with himself and the world. At that moment he spotted Angela, and she distinctly saw a smirk pass across his face as he made a bee-line towards the table at which the three ladies were sitting. Angela opened her mouth to speak, but was forestalled as he bent over, kissed her on the cheek and said:

'Hallo, Mother. They told me I'd find you here. You might have let me know you were planning to go away.'

Angela was too confounded to say a word, but sat with her mouth still open.

'Well, don't just sit there with a face like a fish,' said Freddy Pilkington-Soames, before she could find her voice. 'It's not like you to forget your manners.' He turned to the other two ladies, beamed angelically and said, 'The name's Wells. I see you're keeping my mother out of trouble, and I've no doubt you're doing a fine job of it. Delighted to make your acquaintance. Budge up and make room, old girl,' he said to Angela, who did so without thinking. Freddy sat down and called the waiter to bring more tea.

Mrs. Hudd and Miss Atkinson, thrilled by the new arrival and the possibility of discovering more about their new friend Mrs. Wells, who up until then had been somewhat circumspect about herself, were more than happy to shake his hand.

'How do you do,' said Mrs. Hudd. 'Why, Mrs. Wells, I had no idea you had a grown-up son. You don't look nearly old enough.'

'I married *very* young,' said Angela, with a glare at Freddy which would have caused anyone else to blush with shame. Freddy, however, was quite unembarrassable, and so merely simpered innocently at her.

'Splendid place this, what?' he said, with a wide sweep of his arm towards the large window with its view of the bay. 'Just a little chilly, but I don't mind that. Once one's travelled to the Arctic Circle anything else seems positively balmy by comparison.'

'The Arctic Circle? Do you mean to say you have been to the North Pole?' said Mrs. Hudd.

'Oh yes, twice,' said Freddy airily. 'Unfortunately, we were a little ill-prepared on the first expedition and got stranded on an ice-floe on the way back. We almost had to resort to cannibalism—had actually got as far as drawing lots, as a matter of fact—but happily just then the thing floated within jumping distance of land and we were saved. Lucky for old Carstairs, who'd drawn the short finger-nail. Lucky for the rest of us too, as we didn't much fancy eating him. Far too stringy.'

'Goodness me!' gasped Miss Atkinson.

'The second trip went much more smoothly, though,' continued Freddy. 'We met a tribe of Eskimos and they took rather a liking to us, and helped us with supplies. Terribly friendly, the Eskimo people. They lead a simple life which looks very attractive to us jaded city-dwellers. I was almost tempted to join them, but I'm not especially fond of raw fish, and so in the end I was forced to bid them a regretful farewell.'

He then proceeded to demonstrate how to build an igloo using cubes from the sugar-bowl. Mrs. Hudd and Miss Atkinson watched with rapt attention and exclaimed. Luckily they did not notice Angela, who was regarding Freddy through narrowed eyes.

'Shall you be staying here at the hotel, Mr. Wells?' said Mrs. Hudd at last, once it had been demonstrated beyond all doubt that sugar-cubes did not stick together in the same way as packed snow.

'Yes, I expect I shall be here for a day or two. Mother is always so pleased to see me, aren't you, old thing?' he said affectionately to Angela, who nodded brightly and smiled. 'Now, I'll bet you ladies know all the best places to visit, don't you? I shall expect you to show me around the place tomorrow. No excuses, now.'

Mrs. Hudd and Miss Atkinson fluttered and giggled, and said they should be delighted.

Angela now rose from her seat.

'Come and see the view from the top of the cliff, darling,' she said, in a voice which suggested that Freddy would be well advised to stand at a safe distance from the edge.

'Oh, certainly, what?' said Freddy. He stood up and bowed ceremoniously to his two new acquaintances. 'Until tomorrow,' he said, and allowed Angela to propel him firmly towards the door and out into the street.

'*What* are you doing here?' snapped Angela as soon as they were out of sight of the hotel. 'Have you quite taken leave of your senses?'

'I was going to ask the same thing of you,' said Freddy.

'Never mind that,' said Angela. 'How did you know I was here?'

'William told me.'

'What?' said Angela. 'What on earth was he thinking? How dare he?'

'Don't be cross with him,' said Freddy. 'I rather wheedled it out of him. I just dropped in to see how you were and found that you and Marthe had gone off somewhere without him. He knew where you'd gone but didn't want to say, but I saw he was worried and kept on at him until he told me. As soon as he did I hopped on a train and here I am.'

'Yes, here you are, and as you can see I'm in excellent health, so you can jolly well hop on another train back to London as soon as you like, and stop all this silly nonsense,' said Angela.

'I know what you're doing, Angela,' he said, 'and I don't like it.'

Angela said nothing, but looked away.

'You oughtn't to be here,' he said. 'I don't know why you let yourself be talked into it in the first place, but you must see that nothing good can come of it.'

Angela set her jaw stubbornly, but still did not reply.

'William isn't the only one who's worried about you,' he went on. 'So am I. And I dare say Marthe is too.'

'You needn't bother,' said Angela. 'I'm perfectly all right.'

'Rot,' said Freddy. 'No-one could possibly be all right after what happened to you. I'd be a nervous wreck if it were I.'

'Well, I'm not,' said Angela sharply. She saw that he was about to speak again and went on, 'Look, you may as well save your breath. I said I would do this and do it I shall.'

'But it won't do you any good,' said Freddy.

'I dare say it won't, but that doesn't matter. I'm under an obligation and I must discharge it, or I shall never be easy. Now, if you don't want to make me cross you'll stop talking about it.'

Freddy regarded her, his expression a mixture of sympathy and exasperation.

'I can see there's no use in arguing with you,' he said at last. 'You've obviously made your mind up.'

'I have.'

'Then let me help you.'

'What?' said Angela in surprise.

'If you're really determined to do it, then it's best you get it over and done with as quickly as possible,' said Freddy. 'And two heads are better than one, so why not take mine, such as it is? I've been reading about the case, and I've thought of one or two lines of inquiry that it might be worth while to pursue.'

'Oh, you've been reading about it, have you?' said Angela. 'Then you knew perfectly well I wouldn't come away.'

'Of course I knew. But I had to try. What sort of friend should I be if I didn't?'

Angela made no reply, but looked slightly less mutinous. Freddy sensed a thaw.

'Come now, don't be angry. You know my motives are always of the purest,' he said, and attempted a winning smile which merely made him look like a dismayed sheep. Angela felt a laugh coming and suppressed it. She gave it up.

'Oh, very well,' she said. 'You may consider your duty done. Now, kindly forget all this nonsense about my abandoning the thing and tell me what you've found out.'

'There's not much to tell. I spoke to someone from the Kent police, a sergeant. He was a constable ten years ago and remembered the case well. They were pretty sure he'd done it, especially since they found traces of her in the cupboard in his room. Interestingly, the sergeant said he'd never have thought Valencourt was the type, but they had a number of witnesses, including servants, who said that he and Selina had had a volatile relationship and rowed frequently—even when he'd been away and was home for only a few days. This chap said he had the impression that Selina was a woman who liked to have her own way, although the family didn't say much on the subject.'

'I see,' said Angela. That seemed to bear out what Mr. Gilverson had said.

'At any rate, the police thought Valencourt seemed honest and open enough, but they knew not to set much store by that. Some of the worst murderers in history have been very charming people.'

Angela thought back to some of her own investigations and was forced to admit it was true.

'Did the sergeant have anything to say as to why the family left Valencourt to his fate?' she said.

'No, but it strikes me as rather odd. There was nothing to suggest that he didn't get along with the rest of them, but apparently they were noticeably quiet when it came to the matter of defending him. I can only assume they must have believed he was guilty. Still, though, it looks like a poor show to me. If *I'd* done something beastly I'd hope my own mother would at least make an attempt to stick up for me. You know the circumstances of the murder, I take it?'

'Yes,' said Angela.

'Not pleasant. Whoever did it must have been pretty wicked, don't you think?' he said, with a meaningful glance at her.

She ignored it and regarded him, thinking.

'Listen,' she said at last. 'Did you really mean it when you said you would help?'

'Of course I did.'

'Then perhaps I shall let you. I've been here two days and I'm starting to realize that I haven't much idea of how to go about it. It all happened so long ago, and after all this time it's going to look rather suspicious if a complete stranger comes in and starts asking questions.'

'The family still live at the house, I take it?'

'Some of them,' said Angela. 'Valencourt's parents are dead, but his brother and sister-in-law are still there. As for the other people who were in the house at the time, I don't know where they are now. Selina's brother was one of them, and I think there was a friend of his too.'

'It seems to me that the first thing to do is to think of a way to gain admittance to the house and speak to the remaining de Lisles,' said Freddy. 'I don't suppose you've had any ideas about how to do it?'

'Oh, don't worry about that,' said Angela. 'I've already been invited to go and have a look around.'

'Really? How did you manage that?'

'Apparently I'm going to buy the place. Mr. Gilverson, who is Valencourt's solicitor—and also, incidentally, his uncle—has arranged it all for me.'

Freddy raised his eyebrows.

'So this is what a woman who owns half of Wall Street spends her money on,' he said.

'I don't own half of Wall Street,' said Angela. 'And it's certainly not the sort of place I'd want to buy in the normal way of things. As a matter of fact, I was wondering how to carry off the visit without looking like an impostor, since I have no connections to the area, and why should a woman alone want to buy such a big house? Now you're here, though, perhaps we can pull the thing off. If you must insist on going around telling ridiculous stories about my being your mother, I suggest we use that to our advantage. We'll say your father died and left you a pile of money and you're looking to put it into property.'

'Splendid,' said Freddy. 'I rather like the idea of pretending to be rich. I shall run my finger along the mantelpieces and complain about the smallness of the second East summer ball-room.'

'It's not *that* big a place,' said Angela. 'Roomy rather than palatial, I should say. By the way, have they given you time off at the paper?'

'Just a few days,' said Freddy. 'I reminded them of the sterling work I did on the Camberwell poisoning story, and they had no choice but to agree.'

'And you chose to come down here? You might have spent the time with that girl of yours, what's her name?'

'We shall not speak of her again,' said Freddy stiffly.

'Dear me,' said Angela with some sympathy. 'I take it things have gone badly between you.'

'You might say that,' said Freddy. 'She has cast me aside for another man.'

'Oh, what a pity. She's obviously had some sort of brain-storm and doesn't know what's good for her. Still, there are much nicer girls out there, and I'm sure lots of them would be glad to take her place.'

'That's terribly kind of you,' said Freddy. 'I feel better already. Thank you, Mother.'

'Mother, indeed,' said Angela. 'The very idea of it! You wretched boy, I was hoping to pass for thirty here, and now you've completely spoilt my plan.'

'I'm sorry, old girl,' said Freddy. 'You know I can't seem to stop my tongue from running away with me.'

'I know, and that tongue will get you into trouble one of these days. Still, I suppose I ought to be thankful you didn't call me Grandmother. When you start doing that I shall know it's time to retire and start wearing shawls and knitted caps.'

'Listen, Angela,' said Freddy. 'I've promised I'll do everything I can to help, but you do know we're not likely to prove him innocent, don't you?'

'Of course I know it,' said Angela. 'I'm not a complete idiot. In fact, I shall be astonished if we do.'

'I mean to say, I'd hate to see you hurt by it.'

'Don't worry, I won't be,' said Angela. 'I have a heart of stone. Nothing can touch me.'

'Rot,' said Freddy. 'Your heart is the same as everybody else's.'

'Sometimes I wonder,' said Angela.

Freddy saw that she would never give way, and had no wish to press the point, so they returned to the hotel, where Freddy went to see about getting a room.

CHAPTER EIGHT

IN PREPARATION FOR their visit to Greystone Chase, Angela summoned William and the Bentley down from London. The house was only a mile or so away, but she wished to look the part. William arrived looking sheepish, but Freddy had pleaded the young American's case and Angela had not the heart to reprimand him for giving her away, for she knew he had done it out of concern for her, and so she contented herself with directing a half-exasperated look and a shake of the head at him, at which he blushed, and thus the matter dropped.

'What's our plan?' said Freddy as they set forth. He was wearing a set of execrable tweeds which had caused Angela to wince, but which, he assured her, were the very thing necessary to convince everybody of his credentials as a young man of recently-acquired riches.

'I'm not quite sure,' said Angela. 'It's a great pity Godfrey de Lisle couldn't show us around himself, because it's he I really want to speak to—although, to be perfectly honest, I have no idea how to approach the subject. It's not as though I can smile brightly and say, "I understand your brother was a murderer, Mr. de Lisle. How fascinating! Tell me, do you really think he did it?"'

'Not the most subtle approach, no,' agreed Freddy. 'Still, though, when all's said and done it might be better this way. If we're lucky we'll be handed over to the butler and perhaps he will gossip. You'd better send William to the kitchens to work his charms on the maids. You won't mind, will you, William?'

William was always happy to accept any task which required him to talk to young ladies, and so readily agreed to try and find out anything he could.

'I don't suppose many of them were there at the time,' said Angela, 'but there might be someone who is still with the family and remembers what happened. At any rate, do what you can.'

'Very well, ma'am,' said William. 'I'll do my best.'

They now turned in through the gates and proceeded up the short drive. Greystone Chase was partly screened from view by two large oak trees, but through the leaves they could see the building, with its two grey turrets and its tall chimneys. As they drew closer it seemed to Angela that the house was frowning upon them, and she had the strongest impression of a place in which visitors were not welcome—or perhaps it was just her knowledge of what had happened there which made her think so. At any rate, she was feeling nervous but did her best to hide it. So this was the house in which Edgar Valencourt had supposedly murdered his wife. What would they find out?

'What do you think, Mother? Shall we buy it?' said Freddy.

'Not until we've seen the size of the bedrooms,' said Angela. 'I won't take anything less than thirty feet square. One can barely turn around in anything smaller.'

'I shall make a note and ask pointed questions,' said Freddy, as they drew up in front of the house.

They alighted and were immediately greeted with impeccable politeness by a smart, middle-aged woman, who had come out to meet them and who introduced herself as the housekeeper, Mrs. Smith. Angela presented her with a letter of introduction from Mr. Gilverson, and she glanced at it but was well-bred enough not to appear to examine it too closely.

'Mr. de Lisle is terribly sorry he will not be able to show you around himself,' said Mrs. Smith, 'but he is at present in London on urgent business. Mrs. de Lisle is unfortunately indisposed, but she has instructed me to tell you that if there is anything you require you have only to ask.'

She conducted them through the front door and into a large entrance-hall.

'We understand that at one time this hall was much more ornate,' said Mrs. Smith. 'But one of Mr. de Lisle's forebears on the English side was something of a puritan. He disliked too much fuss and so had a lot of it taken out, although as you can see this carved panelling escaped the destruction, and is considered by experts to be a particularly fine example of the art.'

Mrs. and Mr. Wells agreed dutifully that it was very attractive, and that it was a pity that much of the original decoration had been lost, and they moved on to a large drawing-room, and from thence to a dining-room, a music-room, a library and a smaller morning-room. From the state of the rooms, one might have supposed that the house was not inhabited, for everything was pristine, with not a thing out of place. Even the chair-cushions were smooth and undented, with no sign that anybody had ever sat in them. How could anyone live in this way, wondered Angela. There was no comfort here at all.

'Along here is the gallery,' said Mrs. Smith, as they emerged into the hall once more. She opened a door at the far end, and stood back to allow them to enter. 'As you can see, it is not really a gallery as such, but the light is good and so it was considered a suitable room in which to display the various portraits of the de Lisle family.'

Angela, who had forgotten her nervousness in her genuine interest to see the house, now felt it all return in a rush, for she had no wish to be suddenly confronted by a portrait of one person in particular. Her heart beat fast and she found herself trying unsuccessfully to think of an excuse not to enter. She need not have worried, however, for a moment's glance as they went in showed her that his face was not among the paintings here. She breathed a little sigh of relief and kicked herself inwardly for her own weakness.

'Who is this fellow?' said Freddy with interest. Angela came to join him. The portrait in question was of a man in late middle age, broad of shoulder and imposing of stature. He had a thick head of tawny hair and a beard of the same colour, and he frowned haughtily out at them as though demanding who it was who dared come into his house and look upon him in such a familiar way.

'That is Roger de Lisle,' said Mrs. Smith. 'He died about three years ago.'

'Are you sure?' said Freddy. 'Did they make quite certain of it before they buried him? He doesn't look the sort to be felled by anything short of a passing meteor.'

'He was a very hearty man for the most part,' agreed Mrs. Smith. 'It was a gastric attack from a bad oyster that carried him off in the end.'

'And this must be his son, the present Mr. de Lisle,' said Freddy, indicating another portrait. 'The resemblance is striking, although he doesn't look as though he's built on quite the same scale as his father.'

'Yes, that is Mr. Godfrey de Lisle,' said Mrs. Smith.

'Wasn't there another son?' said Freddy. The housekeeper hesitated, and he went on confidentially, 'We know all about the family scandal from old Gilverson, of course. He wanted to be certain that we didn't care about that sort of thing before we came to look at the place. It's all the same to me, but I thought Mother might be a little worried.'

'What's past is past,' said Angela, who here felt called upon to say something. 'I don't believe in ghosts myself, but if one's buying a place one likes to know everything beforehand, just so there are no unpleasant surprises afterwards.'

'It must have been a terrible time for the family,' said Freddy, adopting his most sympathetic manner—the one with which he had induced many a wronged wife to tell far more than she had intended to about her husband's mysterious disappearance in company with a painted young woman and the week's takings. 'And for the servants, too. We never hear much about *them* in cases such as this, do we? No-one ever considers *their* feelings, or asks how they can be expected to get on with their work, what with people weeping in corners and the police tramping muddy footprints all over the place.'

'No indeed,' said Mrs. Smith, sensing a kindred spirit. 'There are not many people who think about such things, sir. I had not long started here as a housekeeper when it all happened, and I'm sure I needn't tell you that the household was in an uproar for many weeks afterwards. Many of the men had gone to the Front, of course, and so we were rather short-handed, and for some time it seemed impossible to get anything done without one of the girls having to be comforted. One of the maids was so upset that she left without notice.'

'I don't blame her,' said Freddy. 'I'm only surprised more of them didn't do the same. You are obviously made of sterner stuff, though, Mrs. Smith. Are you the only one left now?'

'Of those who were here at the time? Yes, I believe I am,' said the housekeeper.

'I understand there was some doubt as to whether the younger Mr. de Lisle was guilty,' said Freddy.

'None of the servants could believe it,' said Mrs. Smith. 'He was very well liked, you see. We none of us believed he could have done it. We all thought some passing tramp must have got in somehow and killed her. I saw Mr. Edgar shortly after he found her, and nobody to look at him could have thought he was anything but truly shocked and grief-stricken. He seemed in a daze, the poor thing. The servants were quite moved to pity. Not like—'

Here she seemed to recollect herself, and Angela wondered whether she had been going to say, 'Not like his family.'

'Which of these pictures is of him?' said Freddy.

'None of them, sir,' said Mrs. Smith. 'After the trial his portrait was taken down on the instructions of the late Mr. de Lisle. I don't know where it is now.'

Angela had turned to look at a picture of an elegant, dark-haired woman.

'That is the late Mrs. de Lisle,' said Mrs. Smith. 'The present Mr. de Lisle's mother. Sadly, she went into a decline and died not long after the trial.'

'And this must be the young Mrs. de Lisle,' said Freddy.

Angela turned her head sharply and went to stand beside him. She could not help but be curious about the woman Edgar Valencourt had loved, married and supposedly murdered. Her first thought was that Selina de Lisle had been nothing like herself. The girl in the picture was slight and fair-haired, and undoubtedly a beauty. She was dressed in the height of the fashions of ten years ago, and was shown in an informal pose in a garden, standing and leaning with her elbow on a crumbling wall. She was painted in full face, but there was a tilt to the head and a knowing look in her green eyes which spoke of—what? Repressed mischief, perhaps? Angela could not tell.

'Such a lively young lady, she was,' said Mrs. Smith. 'All the gentleman admired her. Mr Edgar was lucky to get her for himself, as she was very young at the time, and you know how fickle the young can be.'

There seemed an under-current to her speech, and Angela longed to ask exactly what she meant by that, but Freddy was already asking another question about one of the de Lisle great-aunts, a forbidding-looking woman in widow's weeds, and so the moment passed and could not be retrieved.

They were conducted upstairs and shown around the bedrooms—none of which was thirty feet square—and then they returned to the entrance-hall, where Mrs. Smith handed them over to a gardener, who was to show them the grounds. They thanked her profusely and went out, and Mrs. Smith was left to wonder whether she had been too indiscreet. The young man had been so charming, however, while the pale-faced lady with the sad eyes had seemed so sympathetic, that she had not been able to stop herself from telling them the story.

They took a short tour of the grounds in company with the gardener, and then returned by way of the side of the house to the front door. As they did so, Angela's attention was caught by a little copse of trees at the bottom of the meadow perhaps two hundred yards away, and she wondered whether that was the wood in which Selina de Lisle had been found. She had half a mind to ask to go and see it, but decided against it, since it would look odd and perhaps even a little ghoulish—for there was no possible reason for anyone to be interested in the place unless they knew of the murder. Besides, after all this time there would be nothing to see.

Angela looked towards the building. Eleven years ago, someone had choked the life out of Selina de Lisle in that house. Whoever it was had shoved her body in a cupboard and then, perhaps in the dead of night, had brought her out here and hidden her in the woods at the bottom of the meadow. What had motivated such an attack?

'Your brain is revolving, I can tell,' said Freddy. 'What is it?'

'Oh, nothing useful,' said Angela. 'It's just that strangling is such an awfully violent way to kill a person. I can't help thinking that whoever did it must have truly hated her at that moment.'

'I dare say he did,' said Freddy. He gave her a glance of what might have been pity, although she did not see it, and then turned to ask the gardener a question.

As Angela continued to gaze absently at the house, she suddenly realized that someone was standing at one of the downstairs windows, looking out. From that distance she could not tell whether it were a man or a woman, but she had the impression of a lowering, brooding face and a kind of stillness. After a moment the face disappeared and did not reappear again.

They returned to the front of the house and were just about to take leave of the gardener when they saw another motor-car approaching up the drive. It stopped next to the Bentley and a man got out, whom Angela immediately recognized from his portrait to be Godfrey de Lisle. He looked completely unlike his brother, having the same tawny hair and light brown eyes as Roger de Lisle, although he lacked the imposing build. He came over to them and introduced himself, then begged their pardon for his having been unable to show them around the place in person.

'Business took me to London yesterday,' he said, 'and I didn't expect to be back until this evening. As it happened, it did not take as long as I thought it would, and so I came back as soon as I could. I see I am too late, however. I hope you have seen everything you wished to see.'

He had an unsmiling, almost haughty manner, although his words were perfectly polite.

'Oh yes, thank you,' said Freddy. 'It's a splendid house you have here. It seems just the sort of thing I'm looking for, and in the right part of the world too. Close to the sea, you know, but at the same time not too far from London.'

'Yes, it is very convenient,' said Godfrey de Lisle. There was a slight frown on his face as he looked at Freddy, and Angela wondered if he was entirely convinced of the truth of their story. She now spoke up.

'Are you leaving Kent?' she said.

'We intend to,' said de Lisle. 'We live here only occasionally. Our home is in France, where we have a wine-making business. Our estates were severely damaged during the war, but we have been rebuilding them and would like to expand further, and so it is convenient to us now to sell Greystone Chase. My wife is French, you see, and is happier at home.'

'Quite understandable,' said Freddy.

They took their leave of Mr. de Lisle, promising that he should hear from them soon, and returned to the Bentley. As they expected, William had not much to report since, as Mrs. Smith had said, none of the present household had been at Greystone when the murder took place. They had all heard about it at second-hand, however, and had seen fit to embellish as they wished. The story of the servant who left without notice had been worked up into a fine tale. It was said that Jemima had always been a little simple, but after the murder she had gone quite out of her mind and jumped out of a window in the dead of night, never to be seen again. No-one had any real information to give, however.

'You didn't say much,' observed Freddy to Angela as they returned to the hotel. 'Are you all right?'

'Yes, thank you,' she said. 'You were doing such a good job of things I didn't feel the need to interrupt.'

In reality, she was feeling somewhat drained and had been only too pleased to leave all the talking to Freddy. Still, the visit was over with now. She had done it as she said she would, and it had not been as bad as she had expected, although they did not seem to have learnt very much up to now. It was still a mystery why the de Lisles had appeared to abandon their younger son to his fate. There was no indication that they had felt a particular animosity towards him for any reason, and so it appeared to her that their failure to speak up for him pointed in only one direction: they must have had some additional knowledge or proof of his guilt, and had withheld it in the hope that the case against him would look weaker in court. It seemed the only possible explanation. But if that were the case, then her continued investigation could not unearth anything to his advantage. On the contrary, it would most likely do nothing except to confirm his guilt once and for all, and would certainly do little to help Angela shake off her gloom. The logical thing to do now would be to step back from the case, but oddly enough the thought of there being some hidden proof of Valencourt's guilt made her even more determined to pursue the investigation, for the events of the past few days had caused a little doubt to creep into the back of her mind. What she wanted was certainty, and to find that she would have to keep going.

CHAPTER NINE

AFTER THEIR VISIT to Greystone Chase, Angela and Freddy agreed that if they were to investigate the matter properly they needed more information about the exact circumstances surrounding the death of Selina de Lisle, and so the next morning Freddy took himself off, intending to go and speak to his tame sergeant in the Kent police, to see if he could furnish them with more details of the events of that day. While he was gone Angela intended to try and catch Colonel Dempster alone, to see what he could tell her about the family. Fortunately for her, Mrs. Hudd and Miss Atkinson had spent a tiring day in Ramsgate the day before, and were just beginning a late breakfast as Angela was preparing to go out. Once outside, she took the path along the cliff top instead of descending the steps to the beach, hoping that the colonel would be a man of regular habits and that she would find him on the same stretch of sand as the other day. She was in luck, for as she walked briskly down the path to the promenade she spied the familiar figure, his dog by his side, strolling close to the water's edge, and she bent her steps in that direction herself, in order to meet him apparently by chance.

As it happened, however, the colonel wanted to speak to her just as much as she did to him. He brightened when he saw her and greeted her heartily.

'Mrs. Hudd was telling me your son has come to visit,' he said. 'Isn't he out with you today?'

'Not today. He has gone to visit a friend,' said Angela. 'He said he would be back in time for luncheon.'

The colonel harrumphed.

'Must say, I was most surprised to discover you had a son of that age,' he said. 'Shouldn't have thought you nearly old enough.'

Angela acknowledged the compliment graciously. He tapped his nose.

'And I've found out what you're up to,' he said.

'What do you mean?' she said in sudden fear.

'Saw you both leaving Greystone Chase yesterday in your car. Was curious, so I spoke to the gardener. He says you're thinking of buying the place.'

'Oh, yes!' said Angela, relieved. 'We did go and see it. My son has just come into his inheritance, and I am trying to encourage him to put some of it into property. He's a good boy, but rather young to have the charge of so much money, and so I thought an estate would be just the thing to teach him some responsibility.'

This was quite patently nonsense, but the colonel seemed not to have noticed.

'I dare say,' he said. 'Did you like the place?'

Angela spoke in praise of its beauty, and he nodded.

'Not a bad old house,' he said. 'I used to visit often before the whole scandal came out. But after Evelyn died it all rather came to an end.'

He looked sad.

'I believe you liked her very much,' said Angela gently.

'Yes, I did,' he said. 'Delightful woman. Don't mind saying I should have liked to marry her, as a matter of fact. Should have been honoured, but somehow I never dared speak up, and then she married de Lisle and it was all too late after that. He took her to France shortly after their marriage, and then I was posted to Africa, although I made sure she knew that she could always rely on my friendship. They came back here during the war when their house was destroyed, and I'd returned by then too, so I began to visit again. Between you and me I could see she was unhappy in marriage, but it wasn't my place to say anything, so I didn't.'

'Why was she unhappy?' said Angela.

'Why, that husband of hers, of course. Something of a tyrant. Never liked him myself. He was descended from the French kings—or that's what he said. He set great store by it, and treated his house as his own kingdom, of which he was absolute ruler. Everyone crept around the house for fear of him and what he might do if he was crossed. A fearsome temper, he had.'

'Dear me,' said Angela.

'Yes,' said Colonel Dempster. 'I don't say a man oughtn't to be in charge in his own house, but there's such a thing as taking it too far. The family had to be careful not to seem to want anything too much, because if he suspected it at all he'd make damned sure they didn't get it, just so they didn't all start getting too above themselves.'

'Goodness!' said Angela. 'That sounds rather mean-spirited.'

'Yes. It was just like him. I remember when Evelyn's mother was in her final illness and Evelyn wanted to go and see her, he wouldn't allow it. Said he couldn't spare her. Of course, in those days a woman didn't go against her husband's wishes, and so she was forced to stay at home and never got to say goodbye to her mother.'

'How very sad,' said Angela.

'Wholly unnecessary,' said the colonel with a snort.

'If she was unhappy in marriage, then I suppose she had to look elsewhere for happiness,' said Angela tentatively. 'What a shame she was let down by her sons, too—or at least, her younger one. What about the elder one, Godfrey? We met him yesterday and he seemed rather a serious sort.'

'He is,' said the colonel. 'I can't say I know Godfrey very well. Not an easy chap to read. One of these brooding, secretive, jealous types, you know. One can never tell what he's thinking. Expect he had a hard time of it from his father. As the eldest he was always destined to take over the estates and the business when Roger died, of course, and Roger was a hard taskmaster. Godfrey quickly learnt to keep his thoughts to himself if he wanted to stay in his father's good books. Yes,' he went on ruminatively. 'I've often thought there's a lot happening beneath the surface with Godfrey.'

'Did he and his mother get along well?' said Angela.

'As far as I know,' said the colonel. 'But her real favourite was Edgar, who broke her heart in the end.'

'If he was her favourite, then his arrest for murder must have come as an awful shock to her. Did she believe he did it?'

'No, she didn't,' said Colonel Dempster. 'Nobody did, to start with. Wasn't the type, you see.'

'No?' said Angela.

'That's not to say he was an angel—he certainly wasn't that. Something of a rapscallion as a boy, I gather. His mother almost tore her hair out over some of his antics, but he was one of those types who could always charm his way out of trouble. There were one or two minor scrapes at Cambridge, but nothing too serious—certainly nothing to indicate how he'd turn out. Marriage ought to have settled him, but it didn't, it seems. I've often wondered whether perhaps the war had something to do with it. I've seen it often enough myself. The number of times I've heard about a chap who went off to the Front and came back a different man—well, it doesn't bear thinking about.'

He coughed.

'I understand they found evidence that he'd done it,' said Angela.

'So they did,' said the colonel, 'but even then his mother refused to believe it of him. I saw her shortly after it all happened and she was almost in despair, poor woman. Was sure someone had faked it to throw suspicion onto him, she said. Roger had told her to say as little as possible to the police, as he thought it would only harm Edgar's chances, but she couldn't understand why he wouldn't allow her to defend her son. When I saw her again next she wouldn't speak about it at all—at the time I thought it was out of obedience to Roger, but now I think there must have been some other reason. She was Edgar's mother, after all, and why should she keep quiet if she knew he was innocent?'

'Do you think she had found something out that confirmed his guilt?'

'Yes,' said the colonel. 'It's the only thing that makes sense. The police had evidence that Selina's body had been hidden in his room, and although that looked suspicious enough, it doesn't mean he did it. After all, anyone can hide a body in a cupboard. No, I think somebody must have seen something else, and kept it from the police so as not to make things worse.'

'I see,' said Angela. 'Presumably it was Roger who saw whatever it was, then, since he was the one who urged his wife to keep quiet.'

'Might have been,' said the colonel. 'Or perhaps it was someone else who then told Roger about it.'

'But who?'

'I don't know. It might have been anyone. A servant, even. They used to sneak about the place quietly enough, and I shouldn't have been surprised if they'd come upon Edgar doing something suspicious and told Roger, who kept it from Evelyn for her own protection at first.'

'But you think he told her about it later? Why?'

'Perhaps to stop her making a fool of herself, since she only knew half the story. Or perhaps to prevent her from accidentally drawing the attention of the police to whatever it was. Who knows?' said the colonel. He tapped his nose again. 'If you ask me, there's more to the case than meets the eye. Still, no matter, as there's no doubt they got the right man.'

'I dare say they did,' murmured Angela. She was reflecting. From what the colonel had just said, it appeared that she was not the only person to have concluded that there must be some evidence which proved beyond all doubt that Valencourt had murdered Selina. And that conclusion certainly seemed to explain the behaviour of the household at the time. If somebody did indeed have further proof of his guilt—what that might be she did not know—then it was entirely possible that he or she had kept the information from the police. After all, it was not to be supposed that his family had wished to see Valencourt hanged, while Mrs. Smith, the housekeeper, had said the servants liked him too, and had not wanted to believe him a murderer. Perhaps whoever it was had confessed what they had seen to Roger, who had then taken steps to ensure that nobody would ever hear about it.

'Ah, it's Mrs. Poynter,' said Colonel Dempster, and Angela glanced up to see the elegant-looking woman she had seen the other day on the cliff top. She was walking her little dog, and she waved to the colonel as she passed a few yards away, although she evidently had no intention of stopping to talk. 'A very pleasant lady, she is,' he went on, 'even if some of the old dears around here are a little catty about her. In a small place like this people tend to gossip, of course. I don't believe a word of it, myself. All right, old girl, go and scamper about in the waves if you must, but don't come howling to me if you get cold and soggy.'

It took a second for Angela to realize that this last remark was directed at his spaniel. The dog ambled off and the colonel bade Angela a cheery goodbye, leaving her to wonder what Mrs. Poynter was supposed to have done.

CHAPTER TEN

A S HE HAD promised, Freddy returned shortly after
midday, and insisted on their going out of the hotel for
lunch, so they could have a nice, long chin-wag about the
case without any old hens flapping their ears at them, as he
disrespectfully put it. Once they were seated in a quiet little
eating-place on the High Street, Freddy ordered a large plate
of chops for himself and dug in with some energy.

'All this wandering around in the fresh air is giving me
quite an appetite,' he remarked. 'I wonder it hasn't had the
same effect on you. Goodness knows, you look like you need
it. You're too thin. Look here, have one of my chops. I'll never
manage all these.'

Angela declined politely and prodded at her own food
without enthusiasm.

'Tell me what you've found out,' she said.

'Jolly fellow, this sergeant,' said Freddy. 'I caught him on a
quiet day so he was only too happy to chat. I told him I was

looking into the case on behalf of the family—which I am, in a way. I said there was some suggestion that Valencourt hadn't committed the murder and what did he think? Of course he said there was no doubt of it, but he didn't mind giving me the facts he had.' He dug in his pocket and brought out a dog-eared notebook, which he put on the table. 'You don't mind, do you? I wrote a lot of it down.'

Angela pulled the notebook towards her and peered at it curiously, but Freddy's handwriting was indecipherable, so she pushed it back.

'So,' Freddy went on. 'They were odd people, these de Lisles. Kept themselves very much to themselves. It was all because of Roger, it seems. He had terribly fixed ideas about his family's importance and didn't want to sully the name by mixing too much with others. I gather they owned half of Northern France at one time, but things got a bit ticklish during the war and they ended up here, with Roger ruling over his foreign court like a petty despot. He was a stiff one, all right. Even when his daughter-in-law had been found strangled and it looked as though his son was about to be arrested, he still looked down his nose at the police as though they were serfs who'd come in through the front door by mistake and trodden something nasty through the house. Evelyn de Lisle wasn't much help, either: she was evidently pretty cowed by her husband and resigned to his having the upper hand in all things. My tame sergeant said that had it not been for the fact that he caught her crying on the day Valencourt was arrested, he'd have thought she was as cold as her husband.'

'But we know she wasn't,' said Angela.

'No,' agreed Freddy. He glanced at the notebook. 'At any rate, these are the events of that day as told to me. As far as I can tell, it was a normal Sunday like any other. All the family were at home, including Valencourt, who had been on leave for a few days and was preparing to return to duty on the Tuesday. The only guests were Henry Lacey—who was there so often that he was practically a permanent resident—and his friend, Oliver Harrington, who was convalescing after receiving a shrapnel wound to the leg, and had come to visit at Lacey's invitation. According to this Harrington fellow, he spent most of the weekend feeling out of place and unwelcome, since the de Lisles were pretty frosty as a rule. He'd only come at all because Lacey was an old school pal of his and they hadn't seen one another for years.

'It appears that Selina had taken her husband's return as an opportunity to make something of a nuisance of herself. The servants obviously didn't like to say too much, but the police understood from what they *did* say that she was a capricious sort at the best of times, and throughout the weekend in question had been behaving in a most high-handed manner and ordering everyone around as though she owned the place.'

'Really?' said Angela. 'I can't imagine Roger putting up with that sort of thing. By all accounts he liked to rule the roost himself.'

'Perhaps he didn't notice it,' said Freddy. 'Anyway, as I said, not much happened until the Sunday afternoon, when Valencourt and Selina had a quarrel. They were overheard by Godfrey and Victorine, who couldn't say what it was about, since apparently it wasn't a raised-voice sort of row but more of a cross-look-and-pointed-remark thing.'

'I wonder whether they were eavesdropping, in that case,' said Angela. 'It seems a bit odd to overhear an argument without hearing at least some of what was said.'

'I shouldn't be a bit surprised,' agreed Freddy. 'Anyway, this all happened at half-past four or so. Shortly after that, Selina came into the drawing-room in an obvious huff, complained to Victorine that she was feeling unwell, and said she was going upstairs to lie down. According to Valencourt, he followed her shortly afterwards and begged her pardon, and they made it up. He then went outside to the stables, where he was seen by one of the grooms, and spent some time with the horses. At five o'clock, Evelyn de Lisle sent her maid up to Selina's room to see if she wanted anything. The maid reported that Selina was feeling better, but was a little tired, and had decided to rest a while. Nothing more was seen or heard of her until a quarter past six, when another servant came to tell Evelyn that Selina was still indisposed and would spend the rest of the evening in her room, and that she did not wish to be disturbed. Valencourt said he knocked on his wife's door at about seven o'clock as he went up to dress for dinner, and again when he went up to bed, but there was no reply and the door was locked on both occasions, so he assumed she was asleep.'

'What time did he go to bed?'

Freddy glanced at his notebook.

'Shortly before eleven,' he said. 'That was earlier than his usual hour, which the police took as suspicious, as they assumed he went to prepare for his trip outside to dispose of

Selina's body. His story was that he was very tired and wanted an early night. He was seen knocking on Selina's door on his way up to bed, but nobody saw him knocking earlier in the evening, when he went to dress for dinner. Between twenty-five past seven and the time he went to bed he was always in view of someone or other, so he certainly didn't do it during that period.'

'I take it the police assumed he did it when he went to dress for dinner, then,' said Angela.

'They did,' said Freddy. 'She was found in the early afternoon the next day, but it wasn't until four o'clock that she was examined by a doctor, who said that she had died at least eighteen hours previously and perhaps as much as twenty-four.'

'That means she must have died between about four o'clock and ten o'clock on the Sunday,' said Angela, thinking. 'And since a servant spoke to her at—what time was it?—quarter past six, we know she was alive then. So, then, the police thought Valencourt did it between a quarter past six and twenty-five past seven.'

'Between seven and twenty-five past, in fact,' said Freddy. 'He was at the stables with the groom until five to seven, then glanced at his watch and left quickly, as he'd realized he was going to be late for dinner if he didn't hurry. His story was that he was grubby after working with the horses, so he had a quick bath first, then went downstairs.'

'If he had a bath, that can't have left him much time,' observed Angela.

'No,' said Freddy, 'but he might have been lying about that.'

'Still, though,' said Angela. 'Even if he was, that still leaves only twenty-five minutes in which to dress, strangle Selina and hide her body. He must have worked pretty quickly. I suppose it might just be possible, but it doesn't leave much room for anything else. What led up to the killing, for example? One would expect there to have been an argument, at least. I don't suppose he just went into her room and killed her without anything being said first.'

'I suppose not,' said Freddy. 'We may never find out. At any rate, we know he had plenty of opportunity to get rid of her body during the night, since it had been hidden there in the cupboard in his bedroom.'

'What did he say about that?'

'Oh, he denied it absolutely, of course. Said he'd been very tired and had slept like a top without waking up once. He said he never went anywhere near the cupboard. But it was easy enough for him to lie about that.'

'True,' said Angela. 'Well, that all seems to point fairly conclusively to his guilt. But since I'm supposed to be looking for evidence of his innocence, I suppose we'd better look at other possibilities. Who else might have done it? What were all the others doing while Valencourt was supposedly merrily killing his wife and hiding her body? Let's assume he was telling the truth and had nothing to do with it. What then?'

Freddy consulted his notebook.

'Very well,' he said. 'If he didn't do it, and assuming he really did knock on Selina's door at seven o'clock and pass on without going in, that means we have a period of nearly four hours, between a quarter past six and ten o'clock, in which someone else might have killed her.'

'But who? Did the police investigate the alibis of everyone in the house? Four hours is a long time, and surely they can't all have been in sight of one another for the whole evening.'

'I should imagine not,' said Freddy. 'I don't know the answer, though. If the police did take down everybody's movements that evening I expect they put the information away in a file somewhere once they'd found the evidence in the cupboard and decided they had their man. My sergeant said he'd told me everything he knew, however, so perhaps they didn't look into alibis too closely.'

'What did the servant who spoke to her at a quarter past six say?' said Angela, after a moment's reflection. 'Did Selina seem normal? Was there anything amiss?'

'I don't know,' said Freddy. 'The sergeant didn't say anything about it—only that the woman had been sent downstairs to pass on the message, and that nobody had thought any more about it.'

'Then she must have been the last person to see Selina alive,' said Angela. 'Apart from her killer, I mean. I wonder whether she knew anything or saw anything.'

'If she'd seen the murder, then presumably she would have said so.'

'Still, I'd like to talk to her. Perhaps she remembers something that didn't seem important at the time.'

'Well, I don't seem to have her name here,' said Freddy. 'What makes you think she knew something?'

'Nothing in particular,' said Angela. 'Only I was speaking to Colonel Dempster this morning and he seemed to think that if anybody knew what had really happened it was the servants— although he's of the opinion that they knew Valencourt really did do it, which of course is no good for our present purposes.'

They fell silent for a few moments. Angela was thinking.

'I can't help feeling that what happened on that day must have something to do with Selina's personality,' she said at last. 'From everything I've heard about her she was very out of place in that house, where everybody conformed. It sounds as though she liked to stand out and be noticed.'

'I'd hardly call Valencourt a conformist,' said Freddy.

'No, I suppose not,' admitted Angela. 'I wonder how he and his father got along before it all happened. I gather there'd been a disagreement between them about Valencourt's going into the family business. Perhaps that rebelliousness is why he and Selina were drawn together. They had that in common, at least. But don't you think it's odd that Roger permitted the marriage at all? With all his concern for the family fortunes I'd have expected him to forbid it, but it seems he was quite in favour of it.'

'According to my sergeant, who knew the Laceys slightly, it was Roger himself who introduced her to the family after he met her uncle, who was an agent or an importer or something of the kind,' said Freddy.

'He must have thought there was some benefit to the de Lisles from it, then,' said Angela. 'Perhaps some business interest. Still, it doesn't really matter. What does matter is that we seem to have reached a dead end. We've spoken to Godfrey de

Lisle—to little purpose—but apart from the housekeeper the other day we haven't seen anybody else who was in the house at the time of the murder. We really ought to speak to Henry Lacey and his friend if at all possible. Perhaps Mr. Gilverson will be able to help me with that. I might go up to London this afternoon.'

'I'll come with you,' said Freddy. 'I promised to see a chap later about something.'

Angela agreed, although she suspected that Freddy's real purpose in accompanying her was to keep an eye on her, for he evidently did not trust Charles Gilverson or his motives in recruiting her to investigate Selina de Lisle's murder. Angela was not certain she trusted him herself, but she comforted herself with the thought that if Gilverson could give her no further information then she would be perfectly justified in withdrawing from the case.

CHAPTER ELEVEN

WHEN THEY ARRIVED in London, Angela went
straight to Mr. Gilverson's office, which was situated
in a small side-street off Chancery Lane, and was admitted.
Mr. Gilverson greeted her with every appearance of pleasure,
and invited her to sit.

'The sea air seems to have done you some good,' he said.
'You have a little more colour in your cheeks than when I last
saw you.'

'Have I?' said Angela. 'I'm certainly finding it bracing, at any
rate—almost to the point of numbness, in fact.'

Mr. Gilverson laughed.

'I understand your visit to Greystone Chase passed off successfully,' he said.

Angela agreed that it had, and told him what she had found
out so far. She also mentioned her conversation with Colonel
Dempster and his belief that the servants knew for certain that
Valencourt *had* killed Selina. Mr. Gilverson frowned.

'Ah, yes, Colonel Dempster,' he said. 'He was an old admirer of Evelyn's. Is he still living in Denborough?'

'Yes,' said Angela. 'He admitted that he used to be in love with her. To be perfectly honest, from what I've heard of Roger de Lisle I'm surprised he allowed the colonel in the house.'

'Evelyn was never interested in the colonel, so I expect Roger didn't see him as a serious threat,' said Mr. Gilverson. 'But you're right—had he suspected anything at all he'd have had no hesitation in barring him from Greystone immediately. He tended to do that with her friends if he thought she was getting too fond of them.'

'I'm glad I never met him,' said Angela. 'I think I should have been frightened of him. It sounds as though he ruled over the place with an iron rod.'

'Oh, he certainly did that,' said Mr. Gilverson.

Angela remembered what Gilverson had said about his having fallen out with Roger and being no longer welcome at Greystone. Evidently he had been subject to Roger's will just as everyone else had. She wanted to ask the solicitor what had happened but something about his manner prevented her, and so she went on:

'We spoke to Mrs. Smith, the housekeeper, who was there at the time of the murder, but she didn't give me the impression that she knew anything and was hiding it. Not that that means anything, of course.'

'I beg your pardon—"we?"' said Mr. Gilverson.

Angela realized that he knew nothing about Freddy, and hastened to explain that a friend was helping her.

'He is a reporter, and very useful for this sort of thing,' she said. 'He can ask questions of people that I can't. He spoke to the Kent police this morning, for example, and found out a lot of information that I shouldn't have been able to get myself, including the times of the various events on the evening in question. One thing I have discovered in Mr. de Lisle's favour is that there wasn't much of an opportunity for him to commit the crime. If he did do it, then it must have been in the twenty-five minutes between seven and twenty-five past, in which he was also supposed to be washing and changing for dinner. That doesn't leave him much time to strangle his wife and hide her body.'

'No,' agreed Mr. Gilverson.

'And if he didn't do it, then there seems to have been a period of four hours in which she could have been killed by someone else. The only problem, of course, is the cupboard. If Selina was hidden there then how did the murderer get her out while Mr. de Lisle was asleep?'

'Yes, that is a problem,' said Gilverson.

'I understand Mr. de Lisle claimed to have felt unusually tired that night, and to have slept soundly,' continued Angela. 'It did occur to me that he might have been drugged to allow whoever it was to come and fetch Selina in the night without waking him up.'

'That is exactly what my nephew suspected, as a matter of fact,' said Mr. Gilverson, nodding, 'but the police were not interested.'

'But then of course that leads to the question of why Selina's body was put in the cupboard at all? If Mr. de Lisle did it himself, then it was awfully stupid of him. But if he didn't, then that leads to the inescapable conclusion that someone did it deliberately to throw the blame onto him.'

'Yes, it does rather, doesn't it?' said the solicitor.

'Did Mr. de Lisle have any enemies?' said Angela.

'That is the question,' said Mr. Gilverson. 'Yes, that is very much the question.'

Angela looked at him curiously, but he did not elaborate.

'There's not much more I can do in Kent,' she said at last. 'I've been to Greystone Chase and talked to Godfrey de Lisle, but I wasn't able to bring the subject up. I should very much like to have had more time in which to speak to him.'

'Yes, I've been thinking about that,' said Mr. Gilverson. 'I'm wondering whether I mightn't be able to persuade Godfrey to invite you to dinner, with a view to buttering you up as a possible buyer of his house. I certainly think you ought to meet Victorine. She's a most intriguing woman, and if she's in the mood she might have something useful to say.'

'I should certainly like to meet them both in their domestic surroundings, so to speak,' said Angela. 'A few minutes is not enough to bring the conversation around to the murder, but an evening might do it.'

'Then I shall telephone him today,' said Mr. Gilverson.

'You'd better tell them to invite Freddy too,' said Angela. She coughed. 'For one reason and another, most of the people of Denborough are under the impression that he is my son and the one with the money.'

'Indeed?' said Mr. Gilverson, raising his eyebrows in some amusement.

'I assure you it wasn't my idea,' said Angela. 'Anyway, aside from another visit to Greystone there are one or two other leads I'd like to pursue. One is the alibis of all the people who were in the house that night, but I'd also like to speak to Henry Lacey, Selina's brother. Do you know where we might find him?'

'I'm afraid it will not be possible to speak to him,' said the solicitor. 'Henry Lacey died about a year after his sister.'

'Goodness!' said Angela. 'How?'

'He was something of a heavy drinker,' said Mr. Gilverson. 'And, as it turned out, an habitual user of morphine. It appears he died from a combination of the two.'

'But wasn't he very young?' said Angela.

'Not more than twenty-five, I think,' said Gilverson. 'I understand he began taking morphine after an injury to his arm during the war. The arm was left more or less useless for fighting purposes and he was invalided out of the army, which is why he was at Greystone at the time of Selina's death.'

'I see,' said Angela. 'I'm sorry for him, of course, but it's rather inconvenient for our purposes too. What about his friend Oliver Harrington? Do you have any idea where he might be found?'

'I don't have an address,' said the solicitor, 'but I understand he was from Canterbury, like the Laceys. You might be able to find him in the telephone directory.'

'I expect Freddy will be able to find it out for me,' said Angela. She rose to leave. 'I'll wait to hear from you about whether I am to go to Greystone again.'

'I shall let you know as soon as I can,' said Gilverson. 'Are you going back to Denborough?'

'No. I think there's little I can do there at present,' she replied. 'I shall be in London if you require me.'

She took her departure and came out of the building. Her first thought was that she had better call Marthe at the Regent Hotel and instruct her to return to London. She was looking about her for a telephone box when she spotted Freddy on the other side of the street, leaning against some railings. She shook her head at him in amused exasperation.

'I knew that story of yours about meeting a friend was nonsense,' she said as he joined her.

'Somebody needs to keep an eye on you,' was his reply.

'You don't need to keep an eye on me,' she said, 'but I thank you all the same.' They turned and walked up the street together. 'As a matter of fact, you might as well have come in,' she went on. 'I've told Mr. Gilverson all about you. He's going to try and get us an invitation to dinner at Greystone Chase.'

'Is he? How splendid. I can't think of anything I'd like more than an evening of stilted conversation with that cold fish Godfrey de Lisle.'

'It might be our only opportunity to get some information directly from the horse's mouth,' said Angela. 'You must exert all that charm of yours and see what you can get out of him. I'll work on Victorine. We'll find something out by hook or by crook, you'll see.'

'I only hope it's nothing upsetting.'

'Nothing could be more upsetting than uncertainty,' said Angela. 'Now, I have another job for you. It appears that Henry Lacey died not long after his sister, but as far as we know his friend Oliver Harrington is still alive. He was last heard of in Canterbury. I want you to find him and talk to him.'

'So Henry Lacey is dead, eh?' said Freddy. 'Don't tell me he was murdered too.'

'Not as far as I know. I gather alcohol and morphine did for him. It's a pity; I should have liked to hear what he had to say about the whole thing.'

They had now reached Chancery Lane. Freddy wanted to go to the *Clarion*'s offices, and so hailed a taxi for Angela, who was going back to her flat. He saw her off with a wave and was just about to set off himself for Fleet Street when he spotted a tobacconist's and remembered that he wanted to buy some cigarettes. Having concluded that business, he emerged from the shop and was about to continue on his way, when he happened to look in the direction of the side-street on which the offices of Gilverson and Gilverson were situated just in time to see a man emerge from it into Chancery Lane and set off in the direction of Holborn. He was too far away for Freddy to see him clearly, but there was something oddly familiar about him. Freddy frowned for a moment, then his mouth dropped open.

'Well, I'll be damned!' he exclaimed. He stared as though he could not believe his eyes, then set off in pursuit of the retreating figure who, despite a slight limp, walked briskly, his head hunched into the collar of his coat, not looking about him. Freddy followed, hurrying to catch up. To his annoyance, however, a group of barristers just then emerged all at once from a building in front of him. In their wigs they looked rather like a flock of sheep, and they had a similar effect on Freddy's progress, for they milled about on the pavement, forcing him to take a detour around them. By the time he had navigated the obstacle his quarry was a good fifty yards ahead of him. Freddy broke into a run, but at that moment the man reached the turning with Holborn and flagged a taxi, which pulled over to let him in.

'Hi!' cried Freddy, but it was no use. The taxi drove off with the man inside it, and Freddy was left standing on the pavement, a hundred questions running through his mind all at once. Had he perhaps been imagining things? Who was the man he had just seen? Had this Gilverson fellow been engaging in some sort of deliberate deception? And if so, why? Freddy remained there, deep in thought. After a few moments he turned round and set off back down Chancery Lane towards Fleet Street. He did not know what it all meant, but he was determined to keep an even closer eye on Angela from now on.

CHAPTER TWELVE

I DO HOPE this isn't going to be a waste of time,' said
Angela, regarding herself in the glass as she put in her ear-
rings. 'I don't know what we'll find to talk about.'

'You will think of something,' said Marthe. 'And I am sure
they will not be as dull as you expect. They must surely be
used to having people to dinner. I expect they know as well as
anyone how to conduct a conversation.'

'I expect so,' said Angela. 'What I really want to talk about is
the murder, of course, but it will look odd if I do it all evening.
I don't want it to seem as though I have some sort of ghoulish *idée fixe* and have merely come to gawp. It's bad enough
manners to bring the subject up at all, but I can't help that. I
shall have to try and disarm them by talking enthusiastically
about the proportions of the house and suchlike in between
times.'

'Should you like to live in such a place yourself, *madame*?'

'Oh, no, I don't think so,' said Angela. 'It's much too formal for my taste. One would be forever worrying about breaking something. There's no comfort in it at all. I wonder Edgar put up with it.'

Here she stopped, disconcerted, as she realized what she had said. It was not like her to be so careless as to mention him familiarly in passing like that, since she usually avoided talking about him at all, if possible. She continued hastily:

'I'd much prefer to come back to London afterwards, but Freddy would insist on keeping his promise to Mrs. Hudd and Miss Atkinson to take a walk with them tomorrow, and so obviously I have to join them. Back to the Regent we go, therefore, at least for one night.'

'Denborough is a very strange place,' observed Marthe. 'Everybody there is old. And it is also full of French people. I do not know what they are thinking.'

'Is it full of French people?' said Angela absently. 'I thought the de Lisles were the only ones.'

'No. There is at least one other lady. She has a housekeeper who is also French and used to be her maid. I met her in the post-office. Her name is Florence.'

'The maid or the housekeeper?' said Angela, trying to decide between two bracelets.

'They are one and the same,' said Marthe patiently.

'Oh, I see,' said Angela after a moment. 'Who is this French lady, then?'

'I do not know. I thought Florence was referring to Mrs. Victorine de Lisle, but then she said something which made it clear that her mistress was someone else entirely. She had to leave then and so I did not find out her name.'

'Perhaps all these French people come to Kent because there is something about the area that reminds them of home,' said Angela.

'Perhaps,' said Marthe. 'It is not the food, however.'

Just then Freddy arrived and announced that they had better hurry up or they would be late. Angela decided not to wear a bracelet after all, and they went down to where William was waiting with the Bentley. Soon enough they were on the Kent road and approaching Denborough. Freddy looked across at Angela.

'All right?' he said.

'Yes, thank you.'

'Are you quite sure you want to do this?'

'Yes,' said Angela. 'And I do wish you'd stop asking me that as though I were your ninety-year-old great-aunt who needed protecting.'

'I don't mean to,' said Freddy, who had been feeling deeply worried and uncertain as to what to do ever since the visit to Chancery Lane the other day, and could think only of persuading Angela to withdraw from the case.

'One might almost take it as an insult,' said Angela. 'First you call me Mother, and then you start fussing about me as though you think my heart will give out if somebody speaks to me. I wasn't aware I'd aged *quite* so much recently. Perhaps I ought to insist on candle-light at dinner, so my ancient and wrinkled features don't startle the servants and cause them to drop the plates. Ought I to have brought my knitting, do you think?'

'Don't be ridiculous,' said Freddy. 'I didn't mean that at all. I'm sorry about the mother thing. It was just a spur of the moment idea—a joke, you know. I didn't really think anyone would believe me. You look quite splendid this evening, as a matter of fact—just as you always do—and not a day over twenty-five.'

'Nonsense,' said Angela, slightly mollified.

The Bentley turned in through the gates of Greystone Chase.

'Now, remember you're still supposed to be considering buying the place, so try and think of some intelligent questions,' she said.

'Hmm, yes—preferably ones that will lead smoothly onto the subject of Selina de Lisle's murder,' said Freddy. 'Any ideas?'

'Not a one,' said Angela, 'but I'm sure we'll think of something.'

They were greeted at Greystone with great politeness by Godfrey de Lisle, who hastened to introduce his wife. Victorine de Lisle was not a woman whom one could meet and forget. She was tall and strongly built—almost mannish in size, in fact—and, as Mr. Gilverson had hinted, was not favoured with any great beauty, for she had a heavy brow that gave her dark brown eyes a brooding, watchful look, and a nose that was rather too large for her face. Her mouth turned down habitually at the corners and she kept it folded tightly shut, as though forcing herself to hold in her thoughts. She was dressed in the style of ten or fifteen years earlier, in a long, voluminous dress; her thick, wavy hair, too, seemed to make no concession to fashion, for she wore it long and styled in a knot at the back of her head.

As soon as Angela met her she had the feeling she had seen her before, and it took only a moment or two's reflection to recall the mysterious face she had seen at the window on her previous visit to Greystone Chase. So this was Victorine de Lisle, then. Mr. Gilverson had called her shy, and her taciturn manner might certainly be interpreted in that way. Fortunately, it soon became evident that Godfrey de Lisle had decided to exert himself in the matter of entertaining his guests, and so the conversation was carried on well enough with little contribution from his wife. He was impeccably polite to her, and continually deferred to her opinion (rarely given), while she was more often than not to be found regarding him with what Angela might almost have called a fierce stare, and hanging on his every word. She clearly harboured some strong feeling towards him, although what it was Angela could hardly tell, since there seemed nothing of conventional love in her expression.

Thanks to the efforts of three of them, at least, dinner passed off less awkwardly than might have been expected, although there was no opportunity to talk about the events of eleven years ago, for Godfrey stuck determinedly to subjects of general interest or discussion about the house. Freddy did a good job of keeping up the appearance of the idle youth of great means he purported to be, and regaled the table with a series of humorous and entirely fictitious anecdotes about the exploits of his aristocratic friends, while Angela threw him the occasional warning glance and did her best to check him when she felt he was departing too far into flights of fancy. Fortunately, this was entirely consistent with her rôle as his mother, and so nobody thought it at all odd.

It was not until the company had separated after dinner, when the ladies rose and retired, that there was any opportunity to broach the real subject of the visit. While the gentlemen remained at the table to drink port, wave cigars around and resolve the problems of the world, Angela and Victorine engaged in their own tête-à-tête in the drawing-room. Angela was nervous, for she still had no idea how to bring the subject around to the murder—and Victorine herself was little help, for conversation with her was difficult enough as it was. Coffee was served and drunk, and some mileage was gained from a particularly ridiculous anecdote of Freddy's which merited further discussion, then for a minute or two the talk seemed in danger of dying out altogether, until Angela suddenly remembered that she was supposed to be there in the guise of a purchaser. She stood up and went across to the window. It had been a clear day and the sun had not long set, and so it was still possible to get a clear view of the wood at the end of the meadow.

'You have a pretty outlook,' she said. 'Very picturesque. I'm glad to see you haven't cut those trees down. So many people's first thought on seeing a tree is to get rid of it as an inconvenient obstacle.'

Mrs. de Lisle acknowledged the compliment but did not take the hint to talk about the terrible history of the wood in question. Angela grimaced to herself. It had been a feeble attempt, true, but she had hoped that something might have come of it. She turned away and set herself to wandering around the room, observing its proportions with enthusiasm. Victorine watched her and replied when called upon to do so. At length Angela's ideas were exhausted and she was beginning to wonder whether she perhaps ought not to come out with it and explain frankly what she wanted to know, when her eye happened to fall on a particularly attractive antique escritoire, on which stood several photographs in frames. Angela bent forward to take a closer look at them, and saw that they were of the de Lisle family. To her surprise, one of them was of Edgar Valencourt. She straightened up, blinking. Presumably somebody must have forgotten to remove this particular picture of the black sheep of the family. She glanced along the row of photographs and saw another of Selina. She picked it up. Here was her chance. She turned to speak, then started as she found Victorine standing at her shoulder. She had approached so silently that Angela had not heard her, and was staring fixedly at the picture in Angela's hand.

'These frames are pretty,' said Angela. 'I was just wondering about the people in the photographs. I seem to recognize some of them. That one is your husband, of course, and that one must be his father. But who is this one?'

Victorine was silent for so long that Angela began to think she had not heard the question.

'She was my sister-in-law,' she said at last. 'Her name was Selina. She was murdered.' She said it flatly, as though she had no strong opinion on the subject.

'Goodness me, I do beg your pardon,' said Angela. 'I didn't recognize her. Of course I saw her portrait in the gallery the other day.'

All the laws of etiquette said she ought to drop the subject now, but of course she could not. She took a deep breath.

'I understand she was killed by her husband,' she went on. 'It must have been very upsetting for you all.'

'It was not pleasant, certainly,' said Victorine. She seemed to have no objection to talking of it. 'This is the man who was convicted of the crime,' she said, taking up the photograph of Valencourt. 'My brother-in-law.'

'I expect it was a terrible shock to find out that someone in the family was capable of such a thing,' said Angela. 'Did you expect it of him?'

Victorine shrugged.

'No,' she said. 'But people are strange. One never knows. Besides, she was the kind of girl who would have been murdered sooner or later—whether by her husband or someone else.'

Angela regarded her in surprise as she made this extraordinary pronouncement.

'Why do you say that?' she said.

'Because she liked to play with people,' said Victorine. She saw Angela's questioning look and went on, 'Even though she was not the mistress of the house she wanted everybody to know that she was the queen, and that we must all dance to her tune.'

'Oh?'

'Naturally, I saw through her immediately,' went on Victorine, 'but the men did not—although perhaps I am wrong—perhaps Edgar did, just a little. He was not the sort of man to be a slave to a woman, and I think it made her a little unsure and all the more determined to win over everyone else. Besides, he was not here much of the time and so did not see the whole picture of what his wife was really like.'

'Goodness!' said Angela.

'It is easy if one is unscrupulous,' said Victorine. 'My father-in-law was a tyrant and ruled over this house, but somehow she was allowed to do things that we could not. He thought her charming, and she had no hesitation in profiting by it. Of course, she did not think it worth her while to charm the women of the house—only the men. My mother-and-law and me she treated carelessly. But it is a dangerous game, that. It is best not to try people too far, because one day they may rise up and *voilà*—' here she snapped her fingers, '—you suddenly find out that you are not as powerful as you thought you were.'

This was the most she had said all evening, and Angela in her surprise wondered what had prompted this awkward, taciturn woman suddenly to become so indiscreet. Perhaps she had never had the opportunity to express her feelings on the matter until now. Whatever the reason, this was Angela's chance to take advantage of the situation.

'Is that what happened, do you think?' she said. 'Did she try your brother-in-law's patience a little too hard? Is that why he killed her?'

'I do not know why he killed her,' said Victorine. 'But she ought never to have come to Greystone at all. She and that brother of hers. Him I did not like. He was always sneaking about the house and hiding in corners. One could not open a door without finding him standing behind it. Both of them the same—always wanting something, always taking something. Take, take, take, and never do they give. That was not the way of things here. We all gave everything—our freedom, our happiness, our devotion—to my father-in-law. Everything was for him, and there was nothing left for anyone else. But the Laceys tried to get more out of us when we had no more to give, and this is what happened.'

'Was there no doubt that your brother-in-law did it?' said Angela hesitantly.

'I do not think so,' said Victorine. 'They quarrelled on the day she died, you see. It was thought that she drove him to fury then, and that he killed her when he went to see her before dinner.'

'There was no question of his having done it later that evening?'

'No,' said Victorine. 'He was in sight of us all during dinner, and then remained in the company of his parents for the rest of the evening.'

'Didn't you see him?'

'No. I went to bed shortly after dinner, as I was coming down with a cold,' said Victorine. 'Godfrey was working in the study. But in any case, the police were quite sure that Selina was killed before dinner.'

Angela glanced at Victorine, but she seemed quite unconscious of what she had just said. If Selina had *not* been killed before dinner, then it looked as though Godfrey did not have an alibi for at least part of the vital period if he had indeed been working in the study. Had Godfrey been one of those whom Victorine had mentioned as having been charmed by Selina? She had talked of the *men* of the house. Someone had hated Selina enough to kill her, and what was more likely to engender hatred than thwarted love? It was a theory which certainly bore further investigation, Angela thought. For now, she decided to let the subject drop. Victorine had given away more than Angela had dared hope, and she seemed not to have noticed Angela's more than usual interest in the case—or her evident prior knowledge of it. It was probably best to stop now before her suspicions were aroused. In any case, it was getting late, and it would be time to leave soon. Angela glanced at her watch and wondered how Freddy was getting on in the dining-room with Godfrey.

Just then a servant came in to deliver a message. Victorine replaced the picture of Valencourt on the escritoire and turned to hear it. As she did so, Angela could not help but notice her hostess's large, strong hands. It would have taken a great deal of strength to strangle Selina, and they had all assumed, therefore, that she had been murdered by a man. But Victorine's hands must be easily as strong as a man's. She had as good as admitted that she hated Selina, and she had spent much of the evening of her sister-in-law's death alone in her room—or so she said. Had she perhaps seen Selina throw a careless look at Godfrey that day and finally been overcome by a jealous fury that could not be contained? Might hers have been the hands which had pressed against Selina's neck later that evening, slowly choking the life out of her until at last she went limp and fell to the floor? It was certainly an idea. Angela looked at the unsmiling Victorine as she turned back politely to her guest, suppressed a shiver, and wondered.

CHAPTER THIRTEEN

AFTER THE WOMEN retired, a subtle change came over
Freddy. He drew himself up and became less fatuous,
more serious, as he considered how best to approach the
coming conversation with his inscrutable host. Now was his
opportunity to draw Godfrey de Lisle out and find out more
about the dreadful events at Greystone Chase eleven years ago.
Why had Godfrey been so seemingly unconcerned at the discovery that his brother was a murderer? Had there been bad
blood between the two? And if so, what had caused it? From
all that Freddy had heard of the de Lisles it did not seem as
though they had been a happy family, but was it all the responsibility of Roger de Lisle, or were there other reasons for it too?

Up to now the conversation had not strayed from general
topics, but now Freddy decided to introduce the subject of
his own family. He waited until Godfrey made some suitable
remark, and then, adopting a wistful air that he considered
convincing, said:

'Of course, Father's death has been terribly hard on Mother. She was very fond of the old stick, although two more different characters one couldn't find. Father wanted me to learn the business—couldn't see the point of my continuing my education when there were factories to run and workers to pay. But Mother was the far-sighted one. She wanted me to go to Oxford and make the right sort of connections. She said that nobody of any importance cares about what happens in the North, and if I wanted to *make* them care, then I must learn how to influence them, and I couldn't do that by sitting in a glass office in Manchester. In a way, she was right: in the course of three years I met any number of politicians' sons; I can name two heirs to earldoms who would dine with me tomorrow night if I asked them; I could snap my fingers now and someone would ask a question in the House on Thursday. But all this mixing with the better sort of company has rather backfired, since it's spoilt me for going back to the business. Unfortunately—or fortunately, depending on how one looks at it—when Father died we were forced to sell one of the factories to pay the death duties, and since a competitor of ours was showing some interest at the time, Mother and I decided that we might as well sell the other two while we were at it. Other than the disrespect to my father's memory I can't say I particularly regret it, since I suspect I didn't exactly inherit his abilities. And to be perfectly frank with you, I'm not entirely sure which would have horrified the Governor more: my selling the business to his rival, or the mess I'd have made of it if I'd kept it on myself. You're in the wine business, I understand, sir.'

Godfrey indicated that that was the case, and expressed some sympathy at Freddy's dilemma. His manner was almost affable, for he had been encouraged by his uncle to try and be more friendly if he wished to sell Greystone Chase, and his efforts in this respect had been assisted by an unaccustomed quantity of Burgundy with the main course, followed by two glasses of Sauternes. He was now completing the process with a generous helping of some excellent port.

'I imagine you were only too happy to go into the business,' said Freddy. 'I mean to say, if Father had been a wine producer I expect I'd have been all for it myself. But steel springs!' He raised his hands and widened his eyes in a gesture that was intended to be rueful and comical at the same time. 'What can one do with a steel spring? Other than cause oneself a painful injury, naturally.' Here he indicated his left ear-lobe, which was ragged and half-missing. 'I did this as a child, when Father made the mistake of showing me how the production line worked close to—I can only imagine with a view to inspiring me with its poetry and romance. "Father," I said, as they mopped up the blood and carried off the fainting women, "I now know everything I need to know about the steel spring. I'm sure you won't mind if I observe the phenomenon from a distance in future."'

'Fortunately I have no such injuries,' said Godfrey, 'but like you, I was brought up to the trade. My father was in the business and it was always understood that I would take it over after his death.'

'Did you never wish to do something else?'

'I was not given the choice,' said Godfrey dryly. 'My father was not one to brook opposition. Like you I was sent to study, but as soon as I had finished I returned to France to take up my duties. When the war began we were forced to abandon our vineyards and come to England, but as soon as it was safe to do so we returned and took the reins once again. Or, rather, my father did,' he corrected himself.

'Something of a tartar, was he?' said Freddy sympathetically.

'He was certainly a taskmaster,' said Godfrey. 'We were under the yoke from a younger age than one would normally expect.'

'We? Do you mean you and your brother? Was he expected to go into the business too?'

'Yes, he was,' replied Godfrey.

'But I expect what happened put paid to all that, eh?' said Freddy. He held his breath, wondering how Godfrey would take his mentioning of the unmentionable.

Godfrey's brow lowered and the atmosphere turned distinctly frosty.

'Not exactly,' he said stiffly. 'My brother had already declared his intention not to work for our father. There was some little dispute about it which as far as I know was unresolved at the time of the events in question. However, it is not a period I like to remember.'

Even Freddy was not bare-faced enough to press further when confronted with such evident unwillingness to talk about the matter, and so he was forced to give it up. He begged Godfrey's pardon and turned the subject, but his host's mood had changed and he had returned to his usual distantly polite self. There was no use in forcing the point, and in any case it was getting late, so Freddy suggested they join the ladies in the drawing-room. The visit ended soon afterwards with polite nothings on both sides, and Freddy and Angela returned to the Regent Hotel. Each had soon apprised the other of what they had discovered—which, in Freddy's case was very little.

'What a pity he clammed up as soon as I tried to introduce the subject,' he said regretfully, as the Bentley turned on to the main road into Denborough. 'I was hoping the drink would have loosened his tongue, but no such luck. He turned to ice as soon as I mentioned his brother, and I can't say I blame him. After all, it's hardly polite to drag up the dead bodies when one's drinking a man's best port under his own roof, is it?'

'No,' agreed Angela. 'I almost ducked out of it myself, but luckily Victorine had plenty to say, as it turned out. I wonder what they're saying to each other at this moment. Do you think they're comparing notes? I suppose the best we can hope for is that they think we have the most dreadful manners. At any rate, I hope they don't suspect what we're really up to.'

'Does it matter if they do, now?' said Freddy. 'Either way they're unlikely to invite us back. This was always going to be pretty much our only opportunity to question them, and *you* got something at least, even if I didn't. Two possible suspects without alibis, in fact. Which of them do you fancy? I should have thought Godfrey was the more likely.'

'Yes, perhaps,' said Angela, and fell silent. She was thinking again of Victorine's strong hands and the way she had looked— almost glared, in fact—at the photograph of Selina. *Would* she tell her husband about what she had told Angela? Or would she keep it to herself? There was something about the woman which made Angela uncomfortable, and although it was more logical to suspect Godfrey, she could not help thinking that it would be better not to get on the wrong side of his wife.

She was still thinking about their visit to Greystone Chase the next morning as they walked along the cliff top with Mrs. Hudd and Miss Atkinson. Freddy was exerting himself to be entertaining, and Angela was required to say very little, which allowed her to reflect at leisure. It seemed to her that it was all very well to believe in Valencourt's innocence (and she was by no means certain she did), but proving it would be quite another matter. What sort of proof could they possibly find after all this time? If somebody else was indeed guilty then he or she was highly unlikely to confess to it, and there were no witnesses to speak up. That being the case, was there any point in continuing?

A loud voice hailed them at that moment and they spied Colonel Dempster approaching them from a little distance away. He had been talking to the two women Angela had met when she first came to Denborough. Jemmy's sister looked as cheerful as ever as she saluted the little group and turned to push the wheel-chair in the direction of the High Street.

'Good morning, colonel,' said Mrs. Hudd. 'I see you have been talking to the Misses Winkworth, as I suppose we must call them.' She turned to Freddy. 'I think we can safely say that society is going downhill when the servant classes are allowed to start booking themselves into expensive nursing-homes.'

'Oh, come, now,' said the colonel pleasantly. 'Miss Winkworth is a pleasant enough woman, and very kind to her sister.'

'Still, you must admit she is not quite the thing,' said Mrs. Hudd.

Freddy wanted to know more, and the two ladies told him of the Misses Winkworth and their impudence in daring to have enough money to afford to care for one of them comfortably.

Angela, meanwhile, was still thinking about the question of proof as it related to the murder of Selina de Lisle. It seemed almost hopeless, and not for the first time she toyed with the idea of calling Mr. Gilverson and telling him she wished to withdraw from the case. It did not last long, however, for she knew she would not be justified in doing so until they had spoken to all those who had been there at the time, and they had not yet seen Henry Lacey's friend Oliver Harrington. It was unlikely that he would have anything useful to tell them, of course, since it appeared he was not a close acquaintance of the de Lisle family and had merely been a casual visitor at the time of the murder. Still, Angela knew she would never be able to rest until she had gone as far as she could, for if it could be said that there remained even the slightest clue, the slimmest lead, the remotest idea that she had failed to pursue, then she would never be able to unburden herself of the debt which had weighed her down all these months, and which she longed more than anything to repay.

CHAPTER FOURTEEN

AFTER THEIR EVENING at Greystone Chase, Angela sent Charles Gilverson a short message to say that she was still pursuing the investigation and that she would let him know of developments, if any. In the meantime she returned to Mount Street and set Freddy on to discovering the present whereabouts of Oliver Harrington, who had last been heard of in Canterbury.

But Freddy was worried. Since that day on Chancery Lane he had not been able to shake off the idea that Angela was being deceived for some purpose that was unclear to him, and so he was less concerned about looking for Oliver Harrington in Canterbury than he was about finding out exactly what was going on in London. Accordingly, when he returned to his duties on Fleet Street he took every opportunity to escape from the *Clarion*'s offices and loiter on Chancery Lane, waiting to see whether the man he had followed would return. For four days he had no luck, but on the fifth his efforts were rewarded, for just as he was on the point of leaving his watching-place in the doorway of the tobacconist's for a society wedding which promised to be particularly dull, he spied the man again, just turning into the street on which the solicitor's office was situated. He wore a thick scarf which hid the lower part of his face, and his hat was pulled down low over his eyes. Freddy followed at a safe distance and watched as the man entered the office of Gilverson and Gilverson, then abandoned all thoughts of the wedding and set himself to wait. After little more than half an hour the man emerged and set off briskly back the way he had come, still limping slightly. Freddy caught him up and walked alongside him.

'Look here, what's all this?' he said.

Edgar Valencourt started and glanced at Freddy, then made a sound that might have indicated weary impatience or resignation.

'Oh, it's you,' he said, without slowing his pace. 'What do you want?'

'Much as I hate to state the obvious, I'd like to know what you're doing strolling through the middle of London in broad daylight when you're supposed to be dead,' said Freddy.

'Must I explain it to you?' said Valencourt. 'I should have thought it was easy enough to understand.'

'Well, evidently the reports were false,' said Freddy. 'But how did you manage it?'

'It's rather a long story, and reflects very little credit on any of the people concerned, so if you don't mind we'll save it for another time,' said Valencourt.

'Then the whole thing was faked?'

Valencourt winced.

'Hardly. They caught up with me all right, but luckily for me they weren't quite as handy as they thought they were. I had a near miss, and seized the opportunity to—er—start afresh, let us say.'

'You call this starting afresh, do you?' said Freddy. 'Coming back here, bringing up the past and tricking people into doing your dirty work for you?'

'I haven't tricked anyone into anything,' said Valencourt. 'I asked nicely.'

'Under wholly false pretences.'

Valencourt made no reply.

'But why drag Angela into it at all?' said Freddy.

'Who else could I ask? Do you suppose I have an army of private detectives at my command? I'd do it myself if I could, but there are several obstacles in the way of that, as you must be aware. Besides, I didn't have much success in convincing people of my innocence eleven years ago, so I'm not likely to do any better now, am I?'

'And you think Angela can succeed where the police failed?'

'I don't know, but at this point anything is worth a try.'

'But why didn't you just disappear?' said Freddy. 'Everybody thinks you're dead. You're in the clear as far as that's concerned. You could vanish abroad and nobody would ever be any the wiser. By staying here you're putting yourself in danger. Why are you doing this?'

'Because, oddly enough, I'd like to have one last shot at proving I didn't kill my wife,' said Valencourt. 'I've done many bad things in my time, but that wasn't one of them.'

'So you thought you'd use Angela to get you out of the mess?'

'Don't you think I deserve justice?' said Valencourt. 'Do you believe just because I'm a thief I ought to be hanged as a murderer?'

'No,' admitted Freddy. 'But we still haven't established to our satisfaction that you're *not* a murderer. I wish you hadn't asked her, of all people. I don't like it, and I'd much rather she hadn't agreed to it. I'm pretty sure she's only investigating out of a sense of obligation.'

'Angela found out, just as I did, that the law doesn't always get things right,' said Valencourt. 'I asked her because I knew if anyone would give me a fair hearing, she would. If she fails this time, then I have nothing more to ask of her.' He paused. 'How is she, by the way?'

'Not that it's any of your business, but she's very well,' said Freddy. 'In fine form, I'd say.'

'Splendid,' said Valencourt. 'Then we're all happy.'

'I don't like it, though,' said Freddy.

'You've already made that quite obvious. Look here, I can't help the deception. Nobody must know I'm alive, or I'll be arrested. But there's nothing underhanded going on. I'd like— not unreasonably—to clear my name, receive a pardon, then retire somewhere far away and preferably warm, where I intend to cause offence to nobody. Is that good enough?'

'It ought to be. It's just that when shady solicitors start sending mysterious letters to people out of the blue, I begin to smell a rat.'

'There's nothing shady about Charles,' said Valencourt. 'He's completely above the board.'

'Then why is he shielding you?'

'I expect because he's fond of me. Is that so hard to believe? He's the only real family I have left, now. None of the others would be prepared to help me even if I asked them. These days I have to take kindness where I can get it,' he said pointedly.

'Then you're not doing all this to draw Angela in again?' said Freddy.

'Certainly not. She's much better off without me. Besides, I very much doubt she'd want anything to do with me now. She doesn't know, I take it?'

'No, and I have no intention of telling her. Just make sure you keep away from her. She doesn't want you and I don't trust you.'

'I'm not especially interested in your opinion of me,' said Valencourt.

Freddy regarded him curiously.

'As a matter of fact, I don't know *what* opinion to have of you,' he said. 'I ought to dislike you but instead I'm finding you something of a mystery. I can't quite decide whether you're good or bad.'

'Perhaps I'm a little of both, like most people.'

'Well, you certainly have the devil's own luck.'

'You wouldn't say that if you were in my shoes,' said Valencourt with feeling. 'The past few months haven't exactly been fun, and I still have rather more bullets lodged in me than I like. I'd have gone away and left Charles to it long before now if I'd been well enough. Still, at least I shall be on the spot if any new evidence does turn up.'

'I shouldn't get your hopes up if I were you,' said Freddy. 'If you really are innocent, then it's going to be almost impossible to prove it. You know, of course, that the one big stumbling-block in this whole thing is the lack of proof, except as it relates to your likely guilt.'

'I'm well aware of it. But I can't help thinking that someone must know something they're not telling.'

'Well, the killer does, certainly,' said Freddy. 'By the way, if you don't mind my saying so, your family are a strange lot. Why did they wash their hands of you? We met your brother the other day and he refused to talk about you. Your sister-in-law was slightly more forthcoming, but she didn't seem to care what had happened to you either.'

'Godfrey hates me,' said Valencourt. 'I did him a bad turn once, and he never forgave me. Victorine cares for no-one except Godfrey, whom she worships for some reason I've never managed to fathom. She hated Selina, who knew it perfectly well and, I'm afraid, set out deliberately to provoke her. I don't suppose Victorine had the slightest interest in what happened to me. The important thing to her was that Selina was gone.'

'But what about your parents? I know your father wasn't exactly the easiest man to get along with, but surely the family honour was at stake after your arrest. Why didn't he stand by you? Your mother, too. Everyone we've spoken to says you were your mother's favourite.'

'Father and I had a disagreement over my joining the busi-ness,' said Valencourt. 'I told him I wouldn't work for him, and I expect this was his way of getting revenge.'

'What? He would have let you hang just because you didn't do as you were told like a good boy?' said Freddy in surprise.

'Oh, they're a terribly brooding, vengeful lot, my people,' said Valencourt. 'It was rather tiresome. It's not my way of doing things, but one had to live with it. If my father believed he'd been thwarted he'd move heaven and earth to get his own back. He wouldn't let my mother visit me in gaol, and I told her not to provoke him by disobeying him. One didn't cross my father lightly.'

Freddy said nothing in reply, but inwardly he was thanking his stars that he had not been born into such a family. They had now reached Holborn and Valencourt began to look about him for a taxi.

'Look here,' said Freddy. 'If it wasn't you who did it, have you any idea who it might have been?'

'I know perfectly well who it was,' said Valencourt. 'Haven't you worked it out for yourself?'

'Let's assume I haven't,' said Freddy. 'Do tell.'

'I'd like to,' said Valencourt, 'but the proof's the thing, isn't it? I don't have that, and without it there's still a small chance that I might be wrong. I don't want to send you off on a wild-goose chase if I am, so if you don't mind I'll keep it to myself for the present.'

'That's hardly helpful.'

'No, but I won't let it be said of me that I influenced the investigation unduly. It might be important when it comes to clearing my name officially.'

This was a fair point, so Freddy let it drop.

'Did someone put the blame on you deliberately?' he said.

'Why, yes, I rather think so,' said Valencourt.

Despite himself, Freddy was starting to believe that Valencourt might be telling the truth. He looked worn and tired, and had the defeated air of someone who had all but given up. It was evident that he really had been injured, and Freddy could not think of any reason why he should have returned to London if not for the purpose he had stated—namely, to make one last attempt to prove his innocence. Was it really possible that someone else had murdered Selina de Lisle?

'You're taking a terrible risk by being here,' he said at last. 'You were awfully lucky to escape—and not once, but twice. You seem to have more lives than a cat.'

'Well, I imagine I'm down to my last one now,' said Valencourt, 'and I intend to be careful with it—unless you're planning on giving me away, of course.'

'No,' said Freddy. 'But not for your sake. It's Angela I'm thinking of. I don't want her to have to go through the whole thing again, as she would if you were arrested. By the way, you're off the hook for one murder, at least. We know who killed Davie Marchmont.'

'Oh? Who?'

Freddy told him, and he raised his eyebrows.

'You seem surprised,' said Freddy. 'Did you think Angela really had done it?'

Valencourt gave a half-smile.

'I was *almost* sure she hadn't,' he said. 'But I shouldn't have blamed her in the slightest if she had.'

'We haven't given the evidence to the police, since it would raise all sorts of awkward questions as to why you confessed to it. Angela wanted to but I talked her out of it.'

'Well, it would rather defeat the purpose of the whole thing if she did,' said Valencourt.

'Quite,' said Freddy. 'Still, we'll stump up the goods if necessary so nobody will hang you for that, at any rate.'

'I'm pleased to hear it.'

A taxi drew up and Valencourt opened the door to get in.

'Were you sorry when Selina died?' said Freddy suddenly.

Valencourt turned to look at him.

'Of course I was,' he said, as though it were obvious, and Freddy could find no reason to disbelieve him.

'You'd better let me know where to find you,' he said, as Valencourt got into the cab. 'I might want to ask you some more questions.'

Valencourt hesitated.

'Leave a message with Charles. He knows where I am,' he said. The door shut before Freddy could hear what he said to the driver, and the taxi departed, leaving Freddy staring thoughtfully after it.

CHAPTER FIFTEEN

FOLLOWING HIS ENCOUNTER with Edgar Valencourt, Freddy decided that it was of the utmost importance to solve the case quickly and thus encourage Valencourt to go abroad as soon as possible. The longer things went on, the greater the risk that Angela would somehow get wind of the fact that he was still alive, which at best was bound to disturb her peace of mind, and at worst might induce her to do something rash. After her acquittal Freddy had been forced to use all his powers of persuasion to prevent her from going to the police and confessing her perjury, and he feared that if she knew Valencourt was still alive but in hiding then all the old arguments would arise once again and this time she would not be turned aside from doing it. Freddy had no wish to see his old friend put in prison for a lie which, at the time, had seemed her only means of escaping a wrongful murder conviction and certain death, and so he turned his attention back to the case

CLARA BENSON

and set himself to finding Oliver Harrington. After spending some time poring over the Canterbury telephone directory and making three or four calls to the wrong Harrington (at the *Clarion*'s expense), he was eventually put through to a woman who claimed to be Oliver Harrington's sister and who, with little apparent curiosity as to why he wanted to know, gave him an address in Bloomsbury and said her brother might be there or he might not. There was no time like the present, so Freddy headed straight off under the pretence of speaking to a witness to a robbery in time for the evening edition.

The building in question was part of a dingy row of ter-raced houses situated in one of the shabbier streets off Gray's Inn Road. Freddy rang the bell and the door was answered by a woman in a flowered apron.

'That'll be that artist fellow you want,' she said sniffily. 'Top floor.'

'Will he be in?' said Freddy.

'I 'spect so,' said the woman. 'I doubt he'll be up yet, though. Always up drinking all night, these artists.'

Freddy glanced at his watch and saw that it was eleven o'clock.

'It can't hurt to try,' he said, and entered.

Inside, despite the presence of the charwoman, he had the impression of grubby paint-work and general dilapidation. The stairs were carpeted only to the second floor, and as he mounted the creaky third flight he looked up and saw a sky-light set into the roof which was so encrusted with grime that it barely relieved the gloom. He reached the top landing and saw a door to which someone had affixed, perhaps with glue, a scrap of paper bearing the name 'Harrington' in faded, hand-written letters. Remembering the charwoman's supposition that the occupant of the flat would still be asleep, Freddy rapped smartly and listened at the door. There was no reply, but he thought he could distinguish a rustling noise from within so knocked again, more loudly this time. At length, he heard the sound of someone approaching the door and fumbling with the latch, then a man appeared. He was perhaps thirty-five, short and stocky, with dark hair and a chin which had evidently not encountered a razor for some days. He was yawning and buttoning up a shirt that gave every impression of having spent the night on the floor.

'I'm looking for Oliver Harrington,' said Freddy.

The man eyed him suspiciously, as though fearing a debt-collector.

'Who wants him?' he said.

'The name's Pilkington-Soames,' said Freddy. 'I'm from the *Clarion*. I'd like to speak to Mr. Harrington about the murder of Selina de Lisle, if I may.'

The man's eyebrows twitched briefly but his wary expression did not change.

'Selina?' he said. 'Why? What's happened?'

'Nothing, yet,' said Freddy. 'But I'm looking into the case. You're Harrington, I take it?'

'Yes,' said the man. He hesitated for a moment, as though considering. 'I suppose you'd better come in.'

Freddy looked about him as he entered, and saw that Oliver Harrington lived and worked in a single, small attic room, for in the corner was a rumpled camp-bed which looked as though it had been recently occupied. The room was a mess, with clothes, old packing-cases, discarded tubes of paint, cigarette-ends and empty whisky bottles strewn all over the place. It was so untidy that it was almost impossible to see the floor, but those few square inches of it which could be glimpsed under it all were bare, grey boards. In the roof was another skylight, this one kept scrupulously clean—presumably by Harrington himself. Directly under the skylight stood an easel on which rested a painting in oils. Freddy picked his way across to it. It was in its early stages, but as far as he could tell it seemed to depict a foreign landscape. On the distant horizon was a dark shape which could not be clearly distinguished, but which looked to Freddy as though it might represent an advancing army, although there was something about it which did not seem quite human. There was a large patch of bare canvas in the foreground with a few pencil strokes on it, but Freddy was unable to tell what it was intended to be.

'It's just an exercise,' said Harrington, at his shoulder. 'I don't know whether it'll be any good when it's finished.'

'Do you always do this sort of stuff?' said Freddy.

'I used to paint portraits,' said Harrington. 'That's where the money is, of course. All it takes is for one or two of the fashionable crowd to decide you're the latest thing and tell all their friends, and then you're set. I thought I could do it—got a bit of a knack for capturing a likeness, you see. But I can't flatter. I paint what I see, and people don't want that, so I had to give it up.'

He went across and picked out a canvas from a pile which stood against the wall, and brought it to show Freddy. It was a portrait of a young woman who in real life must have been very pretty. Harrington had captured her beauty and her youth to perfection—but he had also captured something else, for the longer Freddy looked at it, the more he began to notice that there was a sly, knowing look in her eyes which added a hard edge to her prettiness and made her appear much less innocent than one would have supposed from her age and her looks.

'Uncomfortable, isn't it?' said Harrington. 'I try not to do it, but it *will* show.'

'Do you exhibit?' said Freddy.

'Not lately,' said Harrington. 'As a matter of fact, I'm thinking of giving up. It doesn't pay and I'm tired. I'm not getting any younger and I don't want to be still struggling when I'm forty.'

'I have a friend who takes an interest in this sort of thing,' said Freddy. 'Do you know Marguerite Harrison?'

'I've heard of her, I think. She's a sculptor, isn't she?'

'Yes. She's helped quite a few artists find their feet. I might be able to introduce you.'

'Would you?' said Harrington, and his expression became slightly less wary.

'I can't promise she'll be interested,' said Freddy, 'but there's no harm in trying, is there?'

'I'd be awfully grateful,' said Harrington. 'I say, have a cigarette. You don't mind if I smoke, do you?'

Freddy accepted the home-made gasper offered him and, judging that he had softened Harrington up nicely, returned to the purpose of his visit.

'Oh, Selina,' said the other. 'I don't mind admitting I was a bit cut up about it all. I hadn't seen her for a long time before she married, but I was very fond of her. We were sort of sweethearts as children—nothing serious, of course, but I was at school with her brother, and so knew her very well. But why do you want to know about her? And what has it to do with you? I thought you said you were a reporter.'

'I am,' said Freddy, 'but I'm by way of being a friend of the family, and they want me to look into it. There's just a possibility that the wrong person was arrested, you see.'

'Good Lord! Are you sure?' said Harrington.

'Does that surprise you? I take it you thought he was guilty.'

'Why, I don't know. I suppose I assumed the police had got the right man. It all seemed to happen very fast, you see. Selina went missing, and there was the search, and then they found her, and de Lisle was arrested shortly afterwards.'

'Did the police question everybody else? Did they question you?'

'Yes, but there wasn't much I could tell them. I'd spent the evening she went missing playing the dutiful guest and trying to pretend I wasn't finding the whole thing deadly dull. I think Henry and I slipped off at some point to play billiards, but neither of us saw anything, and the police didn't press the question.' He frowned. 'I haven't thought about it in years,' he said. 'But it's odd, when you think about it.'

'What's odd?'

'The way they all behaved when it happened. Edgar de Lisle put on a show of being shocked, as one would expect, but the

THE SHADOW AT GREYSTONE CHASE

others all seemed to close up, almost. Oh, they said what was proper, right enough, but there was something cold—almost false—about it, I think.'

'You mean they didn't care that Selina was dead?'

'I shouldn't say that, exactly. I should rather say they knew they ought to care and were doing their best to pretend they did. I can't think of any better way of putting it.'

'What about your pal, Henry Lacey?' said Freddy. 'How did he take it?'

'That was rather queer too. He was certainly horrified, but he seemed almost to blame her for it.'

'Blame her? What do you mean?'

'Oh, it was just something he said. He said she was an idiot and ought to have been more careful. At the time I thought it was just because he was upset. People talk wildly when they've had a shock, and it doesn't mean anything. But afterwards, I thought he must have seen it coming. Perhaps he'd heard the two of them having a row, or something.'

'I understand he's dead now,' said Freddy.

'Yes,' said Harrington. 'He is. He died not long after Selina, as a matter of fact. I was the one who found him.' He saw Freddy's questioning gaze and explained, 'We shared lodgings here in London for a while. I didn't particularly want to, but Henry had found a place and needed someone to move into the other room, so I agreed to it.'

'Why didn't you want to?' said Freddy. He was curious to find out more about Henry Lacey, about whom he had heard little so far.

Harrington hesitated.

'Because he wasn't the same chap I'd grown up with,' he said. 'People change all the time, of course, but in this case he turned into something I didn't particularly like.'

'In what way?'

'He'd always been the type who enjoyed secrets. Even when we were kids he liked to find out what people wanted to hide. Then he'd boast that he knew things and could tell if he liked. Half the time it was pure invention, but now and again he'd find out a secret of mine and tease me with it. I didn't like it, but he was a decent enough fellow otherwise, and so we got along and were by way of being good friends. We saw one another less and less as we grew older, and then we both went off to fight—he to France and I to Belgium. Then in early nineteen eighteen I got a nasty shrapnel wound to the leg and was sent home to recover. I was waiting for my orders to go out again when I bumped into Henry in Canterbury, and we had a fine old morning reminiscing about old times. I noticed then that he seemed to have changed. He said a couple of things I didn't quite like, but I put it down to the war. He'd been shot badly in the arm and never fully recovered the use of it, so I could hardly blame him for being sardonic. They'd given him morphine in hospital and he was still taking it, as I found out later.

'We were still talking when Selina turned up. I hadn't seen her since her engagement and I knew nothing of what had happened, so I made rather an idiot of myself by asking about Godfrey. Henry seemed to think my mistake was terribly funny, but Selina told him off and invited me to Greystone

THE SHADOW AT GREYSTONE CHASE

Chase to meet the family. That's how I came to be there when she died.'

'What do you mean, you made an idiot of yourself by asking about Godfrey?' said Freddy.

'Why, I knew she'd been engaged to him, but nobody had told me that she'd ended up marrying his brother,' said Harrington.

'What?' said Freddy. 'Do you mean she was originally going to marry Godfrey de Lisle?'

'Oh yes,' said Harrington. 'I assumed you knew. The wedding was all arranged when Edgar came home and stole her from under Godfrey's nose.'

CHAPTER SIXTEEN

FREDDY STARED IN astonishment. Now he understood what Valencourt had meant when he said he had done his brother a bad turn. And what a bad turn it was! To steal his brother's intended, marry her and bring her to live with them under the same roof—why, it was little wonder there had been bad feeling between the brothers. This was a motive for murder indeed! Everything Freddy had heard about the de Lisles up to now convinced him that Godfrey was not the sort of man to let a slight of this kind pass unavenged, and here, for the first time, was confirmation that there was every reason for Godfrey to have done it. How better to revenge himself than by killing the girl who had thrown him over and then pinning the blame on the man who had been responsible for it all? It made perfect sense.

'How did Godfrey take it?' he said. 'I mean to say, it's hardly the done thing, is it, to run off with one's brother's fiancée just before the wedding.'

'No,' agreed Harrington. 'But they were a queer lot and as far as I know it was never mentioned. Anyway, from something Henry said I got the impression that it was the old man who had arranged the thing with Godfrey in the first place.'

'The old man? Do you mean Roger de Lisle?'

'Yes. He was the one who first met the Laceys, at their uncle's house, and for some reason best known to himself he became fearfully keen to have Selina marry Godfrey.'

'Weren't Godfrey and Selina to have any say in the matter?'

'Who knows? At any rate, he didn't say no, and neither did Selina.'

'She can't have been in love with him, though, if she threw him over so easily,' observed Freddy.

'I dare say she wasn't,' said Harrington. 'But one couldn't blame her for accepting him. They hadn't a penny between them, she and Henry, and the de Lisles were rich. She'd have to have had a pretty good reason to turn him down.'

'Do you know what happened, exactly? I mean, how one brother ended up being substituted for another?'

'I couldn't say for certain, but it's easy enough to understand if you ever met the two of them. Edgar must have been like a breath of fresh air after Godfrey, who was a dull old stick. I don't know how Edgar squared it with his family—or whether he squared it with Godfrey at all, but still, the fact is that Selina ended up marrying him instead of his brother.'

'Goodness,' said Freddy. He considered for a second, trying to imagine Godfrey's reaction when he found out that he had been supplanted. Had he gone to the wedding? Or had he stayed away indignantly? He had certainly not forgiven the affront—Valencourt himself had admitted that—but how far had he taken his resentment? That was the question.

'I gather Henry lived with them all at Greystone Chase afterwards,' he said.

'Not exactly,' said Harrington. 'That's the impression he tried to give me, but from one or two things that were said while I was there I think he rather invited himself to stay—and more often than he was wanted. He'd never been the type to care about things like that, though. He was a thick-skinned sort of fellow and I'm sure he would have quite happily stayed there until they threw him out.'

'Once Selina died he had to leave, I imagine,' said Freddy.

'As a matter of fact, I think he stayed even after that,' said Harrington. 'A week or two later I was sent back to the Front, but I did have a few letters from him with the Greystone address on. I suppose they didn't feel up to getting rid of him, since he'd just lost his sister.'

'Tell me about the night Selina died.'

'Why, I can't tell you much at all. I was in the house, of course, but I wasn't paying too much attention to anything, since to be perfectly honest I was feeling out of place and wishing that I hadn't accepted the invitation to visit. They weren't the friendliest lot, and I couldn't help feeling that they'd rather Selina hadn't invited me at all.'

'Selina and Henry were welcoming enough, presumably?'

'Henry was, yes, but Selina was on her high horse. She seemed pleased with herself for some reason, and was flouncing about a bit and giving herself airs. At first I thought it was because Edgar had come home, but it wasn't that, as they were cross with one another most of the weekend.'

'That's interesting,' said Freddy. 'I wonder what she was so pleased about.'

'I don't know,' said Harrington. 'I expect someone had said something to her that made her feel important. She liked that, you see. She craved attention, and made sure she got it. I knew her of old, so I didn't take it too seriously, but I could see it made the others uncomfortable—the women, especially.'

That was hardly surprising, thought Freddy. Selina did not sound as though she had been the sort of girl to be popular with other women, given her apparent need to draw male attention to herself at all times. He asked Oliver Harrington a few more questions about his movements that weekend, but Harrington had nothing to say that he had not already told the police at the time.

'I'm sorry I can't be more help,' he said. 'But I thought it was all cut and dried. It never occurred to me that they might have got the wrong man. I say, I hope you don't suspect me.'

'Oh, the idea hadn't even occurred to me,' lied Freddy. 'Why, you didn't have a motive, did you? After all, it's not as though you were in love with her or anything.'

'No, I wasn't,' said Harrington a little sadly. 'I might have been when we were younger—just a little, you know—but she wasn't the sort of girl I'd have wanted to marry. Nothing would ever have been good enough for her, and as you can see, I'm hardly in a position to provide even for a wife of more modest tastes than Selina. She was poor and wanted money, and the de Lisles had plenty of that. Much good it did her. Or Henry,' he added.

'Why do you say that?' said Freddy.

'Why, because the money killed him in the end, too.'

'What money?'

'Their money, of course. After Selina died, Henry began working for the de Lisles. I don't know what he did, exactly—something on the import side, he said, although he never seemed to do any work. That's when we started sharing lodgings here in London. I think whatever he was doing they must have paid him well for it, because I'm almost certain he saw to the lion's share of the rent. I have no idea how much the flat cost, because he found it and took care of all that, but the place was just off Sloane Street and it was nicely done up, so I'm sure my share was more than I could have afforded at full rate.'

Freddy's ears pricked up at this.

'I wonder what the job was,' he said. 'Perhaps it was the one Edgar de Lisle was supposed to take. I gather he'd had a dispute with his father and had refused to work for the family business.'

'I expect so,' agreed Harrington. 'I shouldn't have said no to it myself, having seen how little work Henry seemed to do for the money.'

'Shirking his duties?'

'I don't think so. He did seem to spend half his time at home, but every so often he'd go down to Kent—presumably to get his orders. Then he'd come back and drink himself silly and take the other stuff. I saw the way things were going—the morphine had obviously got a hold on him by that point, but whenever I tried to give him a talking-to he'd wave me away.'

'Did he ever say anything to you about what had happened to Selina?'

Harrington frowned.

'Not that I recall,' he said. 'He used to drop dark hints about the de Lisles sometimes, when he came back from Kent.'

'Dark hints?' said Freddy. 'What about?'

'Oh, nothing that made much sense,' said Harrington. 'He said that if he wanted to, he could reveal something that would bring down the whole family and cause all sorts of trouble. I didn't take much notice since it was just like him to say things like that, and in any case he only said it when he was under the influence.'

'Then you have no idea what he might have been referring to?'

'Not really. I assumed if anything it was that the de Lisles were involved in some shady business or other. I wasn't interested in that sort of thing so I didn't inquire further.'

'How long did he work for the de Lisles?' said Freddy. 'You said he died shortly after his sister.'

'Yes—I think it was about a year later. It was a shock, but I can't say I was exactly surprised. The drinking had been getting worse and a few times I had to wake him up when he'd taken too much morphine. I told him to get a grip on himself, but the habit had got him, and he was getting plenty of money from the de Lisles, so he had no reason to stop. In his last few weeks he started talking wildly about how they wanted him dead, but I took that to be the sort of thing someone in his state would come out with. I remember I tried to persuade him to give up the job, purely because I didn't think the money was doing him any good, but he wouldn't. I was right, though.'

He fell silent, remembering.

'What happened?' said Freddy.

'The day he died I'd been out all night—I used to mix with a fast crowd in those days—and didn't wake up until about one. Henry seemed to have a visitor so I stayed in my room and left them to it for a while—I think I drifted off again, as a matter of fact. When I eventually got up I found that whoever it was had left and the place was deserted—or at least, that's what I thought. I went out for a little while and when I came back Henry still wasn't at home, which struck me as odd, so I went into his room and found him there, lying on the bed. The doctor said he'd been dead a good few hours, and there was nothing I could have done, because a dose of morphine even half the size of the one he'd taken would have been enough to kill him, especially since his system had been weakened by drink. Still, though, I've often wished I'd got up earlier that day. Perhaps I might have stopped him. I wasn't especially fond of the fellow, but I shouldn't have wished that on him.'

'Who was his visitor?' said Freddy. 'Did you ever find out?'

'No,' said Harrington. 'I expect it was the chap who got him the stuff. He never showed his face again—luckily for him, as I'd have had some things to say if he had.'

'Ye-es,' said Freddy thoughtfully. He was looking at the matter in an entirely different light. The death of Henry Lacey so soon after that of his sister struck him as particularly suspicious, especially given the circumstances. What if Henry had known something about Selina's death and had taken the opportunity to blackmail the de Lisles in return for his silence? It would certainly explain why they had given him a job which seemed to require nothing of him, and why he had seemed to be so much in funds for the last year of his life. Of course, in the normal way of things one would have expected him to go straight to the police if he knew or suspected who had really killed Selina, but if at the time he had been an habitual user of morphine then perhaps the lure of money had been too much to resist. Was that what had happened?

He thanked Oliver Harrington and promised to speak to Marguerite Harrison about the young artist's work, then took his leave and headed back to Fleet Street. The conversation had been suggestive, to say the least, although it had produced little in the way of solid evidence. It now looked as though Godfrey de Lisle had had a much stronger motive than his brother for killing Selina, and might even have had the opportunity to do it if the killing had taken place *after* dinner rather than before, as the police had assumed. But how could Godfrey's guilt be proved? If no evidence could be found, then the stain would remain on Edgar Valencourt's character, such as it was, and his brother would have got away with murder—a fitting revenge indeed on those who had slighted him.

CHAPTER SEVENTEEN

FREDDY LOST NO time in visiting Angela to apprise her of the details of his conversation with Oliver Harrington. Angela was surprised but pleased that her suspicions of Godfrey de Lisle had been proved correct.

'I suppose we oughtn't to be too surprised at Valencourt's stealing Selina from under his brother's nose,' she said. 'He always was very fond of taking what didn't belong to him.'

Freddy glanced at her but her face revealed nothing.

'Do you really suppose Henry Lacey was murdered?' she went on. 'How can we find out?'

'I shall see what I can discover from the police,' said Freddy. 'His death was ruled accidental, but that's not to say there were no suspicions at the time.'

'Still, we're unlikely ever to prove it,' said Angela. 'This is what I feared would happen. There's just enough doubt about Valencourt's guilt to justify an investigation, but seemingly not enough evidence to exonerate him. I suppose this is almost as far as we can go with our inquiries. I had better go and see Mr. Gilverson and tell him what we've found out—although it's of precious little use. Still, I've done what I promised, and I don't think I can be blamed for retiring gracefully from the case if we don't find out anything more about Henry's death in the next few days.'

Freddy was relieved. He had failed to persuade Angela to give it up, but even she knew that there was no longer any reason for her to continue if they had reached a dead end. Of course, it was unfortunate for Valencourt if indeed he had not killed his wife, but even if they *had* managed to prove him innocent it was not as though he could have emerged from the shadows and resumed his normal life, since he was sought for other crimes than murder. He would forever be a wanted man, destined to remain in hiding.

Freddy went off, promising to call if he found out anything more from the police about Henry Lacey's death, and Angela was left alone to think. It had not escaped her notice that Freddy had been seizing any excuse he could to try and talk her out of the investigation, although she had firmly resisted every attack. Moreover, she had begun to see a worried look in Marthe's eye lately—or perhaps it had been there all the time; she was not quite sure. The thought irritated her. Did everybody really believe her to be such a weakling? Why, she was perfectly well. True, the trial had been upsetting, but she had come through it and, she flattered herself, had been successful in her attempts to resume her normal life. Of course, the investigation into Selina de Lisle's murder was a little inconvenience, in that it tended to remind her of things she preferred to forget, but it would soon be over and then she would be happy again, she was sure of it.

She sighed and turned to a looking-glass which hung on the wall. A tired face looked out at her and she grimaced at it, then spent some time examining herself dispassionately. Marthe was right: all this travelling about did little for the complexion, and Angela felt she was looking distinctly peaky. Perhaps she ought to have taken her maid's advice and gone somewhere warm on the Continent. Or there was always the States. She had received a letter from her American lawyer that morning about the sale of Bernstein & Associates. The terms were acceptable to the buyer, he said, but there were one or two points that merited further discussion, and it would be better if she were there to attend to them in person. But how could she concentrate on business abroad when there were matters still to resolve here?

Somewhat irrationally, given her rejection of Freddy's attempts to get her off the case, she would have been only too glad to find a good excuse to give it up, and she felt a little relieved at the thought that she would shortly be able to withdraw with a clear conscience. She had done all she could, and nobody could say she had not tried her hardest. Very soon she could resume her efforts to forget the past few months, as she had been doing before Mr. Gilverson sent his letter. The investigation had been an uncomfortable experience, but she had no intention of allowing it to disturb her peace of mind any more than necessary. Of course she had been foolish—she had admitted as much to Freddy after the trial—but she was certainly not foolish enough to mourn a man who had been so eminently unsuitable in every way, whether he had murdered his wife or not. It had been an attraction on her part which had been most unlike her, and for which she never ceased to chide herself. As for him, if he wanted to go around confessing to murders he had not committed—well, that was entirely his own affair. She had not asked him to do it, and could not possibly be held responsible for the consequences. That was the right way to look at it, she told herself, and for a moment she *almost* managed to believe it. That would have to do for the present, but she was sure it would become easier as time passed. Now all she had to do was to convince her friends that there was no need to worry about her, as they evidently did. It was kind of them, but entirely pointless, since of course there was nothing at all wrong with her.

'I am perfectly all right,' she said firmly to her reflection, and pasted on a bright smile.

Nonetheless, she was still feeling out of sorts as she went to see Mr. Gilverson. The solicitor greeted her with his usual impeccable courtesy and was only too keen to hear what she had to report. He raised his eyebrows when Angela mentioned her suspicions about Godfrey's motive.

'Ah, of course,' he said. 'I must confess I had forgotten about that particular incident, since Godfrey married Victorine not long after his engagement with Selina came to an end and the thing was, of course, never mentioned within the family. Edgar had the decency not to boast about it, at least. I'm not quite sure how it all happened, but yes, I believe there was a certain amount of resentment on Godfrey's part.'

'Enough for him to wish them dead, do you think?' said Angela.

Mr. Gilverson considered.

'Perhaps,' he said. 'He is very like his father in many respects, and has a tendency to hold a grudge. Yes, I can see why one might be suspicious of him.'

'And it seems he may have no alibi,' said Angela. 'He *or* his wife, in fact. According to Victorine, he spent much of the evening alone in the study, while she went to bed early as she was coming down with a cold. Either of them might have done it some time after dinner and hidden Selina's body in the cupboard.'

'Oh, you suspect Victorine too, do you?'

'She disliked Selina,' said Angela, 'and she certainly looks as though she has the physical strength to have done it, although I can't think of a reason why she would want to pin the blame deliberately on her brother-in-law, as she didn't seem to have any particular animosity towards him. I think Godfrey is the more likely of the two, but I shouldn't rule out his wife. Then there is the matter of Henry Lacey.'

'Yes,' said Gilverson. 'Now that is a surprise to me, since the possibility of murder was never suggested at the time, as far as I know. Do you think the visitor Harrington heard might have been someone Lacey knew from Kent?'

'It's possible. Freddy certainly thinks it might have been. He is going to speak to the police and see what they have to say about it. Of course, even if it turns out that there is some doubt, then we are in the same position as with the murder of Selina, since we have no proof. Henry Lacey certainly died of an overdose of morphine, but there is no way of finding out whether he took it himself or whether it was administered deliberately by someone else. It's all very well having suspicions, but I'm afraid that simply won't be good enough for the Home Office, which is not going to reopen an investigation on such flimsy grounds.'

'Yes, I think you're right,' said Mr. Gilverson.

'So I'm afraid this is where it ends,' said Angela, and with those words felt a sudden rush of relief. 'Unless Freddy gets another lead from Henry's death then there's nothing more I can do. It's all been quite unsatisfactory, to tell the truth. I feel as though I've been chasing around in circles and have nothing much to show for it except suspicions. On this occasion I think I must admit defeat.'

'You've proved nothing, true,' said Mr. Gilverson. 'But please answer me frankly, Mrs. Marchmont: from what you have learned so far, do you believe he did it?'

Angela hesitated.

'I think there's a good chance he didn't,' she said slowly at last. 'But if you want my honest opinion I'd say it would be better to leave it now, after all this time. There's simply no way of proving what happened. I suppose I could try and track down every single servant who was in the house eleven years ago, but even then what good would it do? The police spoke to them at the time. None of them was in that part of the house when Selina died—or at least, none of them saw anything.'

Here she frowned, as an errant thought flitted into her head. What was it? Something Colonel Dempster had said, perhaps?

'No,' said Gilverson. 'I agree that would be a waste of your time, and I shouldn't dream of asking you to do it.' Here he paused, and seemed to be thinking. 'It has, however, just occurred to me that there is a person I forgot to mention when we spoke initially about the case. She was a friend of the family, and was living in Denborough at the time, and I wonder whether she might be able to tell you something—always assuming she is still there.'

Angela looked up and found him gazing at her speculatively. It was an expression she had often seen on the face of Edgar Valencourt, and it had invariably meant he was up to something. A wave of suspicion washed over her.

'Who is she?' she said.

'She is a French lady by the name of Mme. Charbonnet,' said Mr. Gilverson. 'She was a young widow who had been a friend of the de Lisles in Rheims. When they came to Kent she followed them not long afterwards and moved into a cottage in the area.'

There was a pause as they regarded one another.

'A friend of the family, you say?' said Angela. 'The whole family, do you mean?'

'Well, perhaps more a particular friend of Roger's,' said Mr. Gilverson carefully.

'I see,' said Angela. 'And you believe she may know something about the murder?'

'Perhaps,' said Mr. Gilverson. 'I cannot tell. She was not in the house at the time, but it might be worth asking her, don't you think?'

Angela was becoming increasingly wary. She could not quite say why, but she sensed deception.

'Why did you not mention this Mme. Charbonnet before?' she said. 'Had I known about her I might have tried to find her when I went to Denborough.'

'To be perfectly truthful, I had forgotten all about her until now,' said Mr. Gilverson.

'Was she questioned after the murder?' said Angela.

'I do not believe so,' said Mr. Gilverson. He coughed. 'She was not exactly on visiting terms at Greystone, and indeed her presence in Denborough was not officially acknowledged by the family, if you understand my meaning.'

'I believe I do,' said Angela.

'Since she was not in the house at the time, there was no reason for her to be brought into the thing at all, but as I say, she knew the family, and if she is still living in the town it is possible that she may be able to tell you something that the police missed.'

Angela was beginning to feel some irritation, for she was almost certain she had not been told the whole truth. She did not believe for a second Mr. Gilverson's story that he had only now remembered the existence of Mme. Charbonnet. She was intimately connected with the de Lisles, so why had he not mentioned her before? The relief Angela had felt only moments earlier at the idea of retiring from the case now dissipated, and her heart sank at the prospect of another trip to Denborough in search of this woman, who had presumably been Roger de Lisle's mistress. But what could Mme. Charbonnet tell her? Since she had evidently been maintained discreetly in a separate establishment she would not have been present at Greystone Chase when Selina de Lisle died, so could not be counted as a witness. What, then, was the use in speaking to her? And how was Angela meant to approach her? It was a distasteful task altogether.

She was about to ask something else when she again caught sight of Mr. Gilverson looking at her, and at that moment he reminded her so much of Valencourt that the irritation intensified into something like anger, and she suddenly saw the absurdity of the whole situation. Why was she doing this? Why was she punishing herself in this way by investigating a murder on behalf of a man who was dead and could never appreciate it or benefit from it? It was too much, and at that moment she decided that she wanted no more of it. She lifted her chin.

'Mr. Gilverson,' she said frostily. 'I have done what you asked of me, and looked into this matter to the best of my ability. I did this on the tacit understanding that you would deal with me fairly and honourably, but it is now becoming clear to me that you have not kept your side of the bargain. You have withheld information from me and produced it only now, when I had begun to feel myself justifiably released from my obligations. So you want to send me scurrying down to Kent in search of a dead man's mistress, is that it? And if I speak to her, what next? Is there someone else you have forgotten to mention? I cannot help but feel that I am being drawn in—that there is some ulterior motive behind your request, or something you are not telling me.'

'I am sorry you feel this way,' said Mr. Gilverson, 'but I assure you I have kept nothing from you that will help our case.

From the start we have been concerned with finding evidence that will stand up in court, and for that it is vital we employ someone who can approach the investigation with an open mind, rather than burdened with preconceived ideas.'

'"We?"' said Angela. 'I understood you were acting alone.'

'Yes, I beg your pardon—of course I meant I.'

'Are you quite sure of that?' said Angela, who was now working herself up into a fine temper which inclined towards the irrational. 'Because if I didn't know better, I'd say Edgar was still alive and doing this to make a fool of me yet again. Supposing I do find some evidence and prove him not guilty, what then? Will I receive yet another letter from beyond the grave asking me to absolve him of all his other crimes too? Does he want me to make reparation for all those things he stole? What else did he leave undone? Are there any library books he needs me to return? Perhaps a tailor's bill left unpaid? So convenient to have someone to hand to clear up all the mess one leaves behind, don't you think? And it seems I'm that someone. Well, I've done all I can and I have precious little to show for it, so there's no use at all in my carrying on. You may speak to this woman if you like, but I see no point in it myself, so I'm sure you'll forgive me if I decline to do it and withdraw from the case. Goodbye, Mr. Gilverson.'

And with that, she stood up and sailed out before Mr. Gilverson could say a word.

CHAPTER EIGHTEEN

AFTER ANGELA HAD left, Mr. Gilverson sat for a minute or two rubbing his chin, then rose and opened a door.

'You can come out now,' he said.

Edgar Valencourt came out of the little side-office to which he had retreated on Angela's arrival.

'You might have said you were expecting her,' he said.

'I wasn't,' said Gilverson. 'She turned up unannounced. Well, that, as they say, has gone and done it. I take it you heard it all. If you'll pardon my saying so, she seems somewhat annoyed at you. Is that a customary state of affairs?'

'More or less,' admitted Valencourt.

'Interesting,' said Gilverson. 'She struck me as a cool one, but that's the first sign of any emotion I've seen in her. Perhaps she's not as unfeeling as she appears. Still, it's a pity you didn't think to mention this woman of Roger's earlier. It did rather look as though I'd been withholding the information.'

'I'd forgotten all about her until the other day,' said Valencourt. 'She was meant to be discreetly ignored, just like everything else in our family. I don't even know if she still lives in Denborough. I dare say she returned to France long ago.'

'Well, it looks as though you'll have to speak to her yourself, now that your Angela has taken herself off in a huff.'

'She'll be back,' said Valencourt, although there was a trace of doubt in his expression.

'Are you quite certain of that?' said his uncle. 'She was angry enough. And she has every reason to keep away. As she said herself, her helping you at all looks suspicious, and I don't suppose she wants to be tried for perjury, as she will be if anybody puts two and two together. Even if she knew you were still alive I expect she'd be far too concerned with saving her own skin to care about saving yours.'

'Angela's not like that,' said Valencourt. 'I'd bet my life on it.'

'I rather thought you already had,' said Gilverson. He regarded his nephew with something like fond exasperation. 'You and your tendency to lose your head over women. You really ought to keep well away from them. Look what happened when you lost your head over Selina.'

'I assure you it hadn't escaped my attention,' said Valencourt dryly.

'And now this one. She killed her husband and made you confess to it.'

'She didn't make me confess. And I have it on good authority that she didn't kill him either.'

'Oh? I must say, she didn't strike me as the type, but one never knows. Still, I must say it was something of a gesture on your part. I can't quite decide whether you're a hero or a fool.'

'I rather wonder myself,' said Valencourt. 'It was an idiotic thing to do, I know.'

Gilverson smiled.

'You saved her life,' he said. 'You're a better man than you think you are, my boy, but you really ought to stay away from women. They've always been your downfall.'

'That's true enough,' said Valencourt. 'Still, I'd like to be sure Angela's all right.'

Perhaps there was a particular note to his voice, for Gilverson darted a sharp glance at him.

'I do hope you're not planning on giving yourself away,' he said. 'It was just your bad luck that young fellow happened to see you, but the more people who know the more likely it is you'll be caught, and that would be such a pity now that you have the opportunity to start again. Are you quite sure he won't tell, incidentally?'

'I think so,' said Valencourt. 'He knows well enough what's at stake.'

'Quite apart from anything else, I'd be in trouble myself if they found you, since I'm the one who supposedly identified your body,' said Gilverson. 'Convenient for you that so many people seem to end up in the Seine, of course, but I'm an old man now and the last thing I want is to spend my declining years in gaol if somebody realizes the truth.'

'Don't worry, you won't,' said Valencourt, with the ghost of his old smile. 'If it comes to the worst you can come abroad with me.'

'Good heavens!' said Gilverson. 'I can't think of anything I'd like less. If you have any care for me at all, you'll stay well hidden.'

'I intend to,' said Valencourt. 'As you say, this is the perfect opportunity to begin again far away from here. It would be ridiculous to throw that away for the sake of a woman, even supposing she could stand the sight of me.'

'Silly creatures, women,' said Gilverson. 'Although I must say this one of yours seems to have something about her. She didn't give you away in court, which demonstrates some sense of loyalty, at least.'

'Yes,' said Valencourt. He looked as though he were about to say something else, but then thought better of it.

'By the way, she seems to think it was Godfrey who did it,' said Gilverson.

'Does she? Perhaps it was.'

The two men looked at one another.

'What if there is no proof?' said Gilverson at last. 'It's all been guess-work up to now, but what if nothing can be found?'

'Oh, I'm quite resigned to that,' said Valencourt. 'I'll go to South America as I always meant to, and that will be that.'

'That will be that,' repeated the other. 'It will be a pity, though. Shouldn't you like to clear your name at last?'

'Of course I should,' said Valencourt. 'That's what this is all about, after all. But there are certain advantages to remaining guilty in the eyes of the law.'

'Such as what?'

'Why, the fact that it prevents me from doing anything rash. If I were in no danger of hanging then I might be tempted to—' He stopped, then went on hurriedly. 'I might become careless, that's all.'

'I do hope you're not going to lose your head again,' said Gilverson.

'Certainly not,' said Valencourt. 'Whatever gave you that idea?'

'She's gone, anyway,' said Gilverson, 'and if she has any sense she won't come back.'

'She will,' said Valencourt, even as the look of doubt flickered across his face again. 'You'll see.'

CHAPTER NINETEEN

B Y THE TIME Angela arrived home her anger had cooled
considerably, and she was feeling not a little foolish after
her outburst in Mr. Gilverson's office. She could not remember
exactly what she had said to him, but one or two of her more
ridiculous remarks remained fresh and clear in her mind, and
she blushed at the thought of them. She felt particularly idiotic
at having voiced the suspicion that Edgar Valencourt was still
alive. It had been nothing but a wild accusation which she did
not believe in the slightest, but it was odd that the thought
had crossed her mind at all. It must have been the uncanny
resemblance between him and his uncle, which had made her
feel quite uncomfortable from the start. Still, even if she had
made a fool of herself, there was no need to see Mr. Gilverson
again now that she had withdrawn from the case. And it really
was time, she told herself. She had done what she promised,
looked into all the clues and arrived at nothing but a series of

dead ends. Gilverson's sudden mention of this Mme. Charbonnet had been nothing but an attempt to keep her pursuing the investigation, but it must have been futile, as what could the woman possibly have to say? Why, Angela might as well question the grocer's boy, or Mrs. Hudd, or anyone else in Denborough, for all she was likely to know. No; she had been perfectly justified in stepping down. The stain on Valencourt's character would simply have to remain, whether he had done it or not; and in any case, it was not as though he had been a good man in other respects—far from it, in fact. He had blemished his own reputation, and what was one extra crime to his name on top of everything else he had done?

So Angela told herself as she sat by the window in her flat, gazing unseeing out onto the street below. She had been absolutely in the right to do as she did. She had tried to pay off her debt to Edgar Valencourt, but the investigation had achieved nothing except to disturb her fragile peace of mind, and it was high time to retire. Of course, in order to convince herself that her conscience was now clear, she had to ignore certain inconvenient facts—one of which was that she knew perfectly well from Marthe that there was a French lady living in Denborough, who would presumably be fairly easy to trace. Another was the arrival on the scene of a definite suspect in the shape of Godfrey de Lisle, who had had the strongest of motives for killing Selina and blaming the murder on his brother. And there were many questions still unanswered, too. Colonel Dempster had said he believed someone in the house had evidence of Valencourt's guilt, but that Roger had initially kept it from his wife in order to protect her from the knowledge that her favourite son was a murderer. However, from what Angela had heard of Roger, that was not like him at all. On the contrary, given his jealous temperament she would have thought him more likely to torment Evelyn with the information in revenge for the fact—real or imagined—that her love for her younger son was greater than her love for her husband. But what if the colonel were wrong? What if Roger had not withheld evidence of his younger son's guilt at all? What if it was *Godfrey*, the favourite elder son, he was protecting? Had Roger known or guessed that the dutiful Godfrey was the murderer, and allowed the blame to be transferred to Edgar? Perhaps he had led Evelyn to believe that Edgar was guilty. That would explain why he had told her to keep quiet, and why she had obeyed. And where did Henry Lacey come in? Had he been blackmailing Godfrey until the de Lisles tired of the burden and disposed of him?

So many questions. Angela turned them over in her mind for some time, then had to remind herself that she had withdrawn from the case and that it was no longer anything to do with her. But try as she might, she was unable to prevent her mind from drifting back repeatedly to the mystery. All other considerations aside, she hated to leave business unfinished, and this was the first time she had ever failed to see a case through to the end. She would have to find something else to occupy herself, she decided, or she would go mad.

Fortunately for Angela, she was expecting a visit from Barbara, who duly arrived, gave her usual noisy greeting, dropped all her things on the floor and threw herself into a chair, declaring that it was such a relief to be free of that dreadful prison for a few days. If anything was likely to take Angela's mind off her troubles, it was the mess and disruption caused to an elegant and well-appointed existence by a fourteen-year-old girl, and so she welcomed her daughter with more than usual gladness. They were to go to the theatre and the shops and the zoo, and they would have a jolly time together, and Angela would be so distracted and amused by Barbara's antics that she would have no opportunity to brood over the worries caused by her own unwise entanglements. And so it proved. They spent a long weekend in one another's company, and Angela began to feel the cares lift from her shoulders as she listened to Barbara's stories of school, commiserated over her scrapes (always accidental), and altogether felt herself being influenced for the better by her daughter's uncomplicated approach to life.

After a day or two Angela decided to introduce a subject that she feared might prove tricky.

'By the way, I've decided to sell the company, so I'll have to go to New York for a little while,' she said one morning over breakfast.

Barbara looked up from her porridge.

'Oh?' she said. 'How long are you going for?'

'I don't know,' said Angela, 'but lately I've found myself rather missing the place. Of course I'm not going to leave you—don't worry about that. As a matter of fact, I was wondering how you'd feel about coming with me.'

'To America?' said Barbara. She considered the suggestion. 'But what about school? All my friends are here. I shouldn't like to leave them.'

'No, but it wouldn't have to be forever. You can always come back to university in England in a few years if you still have your heart set on Cambridge, although of course many American colleges are very good too. Look here.' She handed Barbara something which had just arrived in the post. 'This school has an excellent reputation. I thought it might be just your sort of thing.'

'A prospectus!' said Barbara. 'I say, you really have been thinking seriously about this, haven't you? That must mean you want to return for good.'

'I'm not sure yet, but I'm considering it,' said Angela.

'But what if I don't want to go?'

'Then we won't,' said Angela. 'Although I'll still have to make the visit if I want to sell the company. But that will only be for a few weeks.'

Barbara regarded her mother across the breakfast-table.

'You poor dear,' she said unexpectedly. 'It's been pretty hard on you, hasn't it? I mean, the trial and all that. I expect I'd want to get away from everything too if I were in your position. It's just lucky for you that you have somewhere to run away to if you can't face things here any more.'

She meant nothing pointed by the remark, but Angela was disconcerted. *Was* she running away? Was that what it looked like? Angela had never considered herself a coward, but now she began to see things in a new light—not just her impending flight from England, but also her withdrawal from the murder investigation. Of course the trip to New York was unavoidable, and there was no reason why she should not stay for a while if she and Barbara were happier there, but the de

Lisle case was another matter altogether. She forced herself to look at the question dispassionately, and could not escape the inevitable conclusion that here she really could be accused of cowardice. There was no getting around the fact that she had allowed her personal feelings to get in the way of the investigation. She had promised to find out the truth if it were at all possible, and yet here she was, declaring she would not go on, when there were many questions still to answer and at least one possible witness still to trace. She had herself admitted the possibility that Edgar Valencourt might be innocent, and yet she had seized upon the flimsiest of excuses to back out, purely because the thought of him brought back all her feelings of guilt at having betrayed him. Was that really how she wanted it to end? Did she want to spend the rest of her days haunted by the knowledge that she might have cleared his name had she only tried a little harder?

'Are you all right, Angela?' said Barbara. 'I've asked you three times to pass the teapot. What's the matter?'

Angela roused herself.

'Nothing,' she said, and helped Barbara to tea. 'I just thought of something, that's all. Thank you,' she added.

'I *said* thank you.'

'No, I meant thank you for what you just said. You've made me realize I'm being an awful coward about something.'

'That's not like you,' said Barbara. 'What is it?'

'Just something I was trying to avoid. But I'm afraid it's unavoidable.'

'Oh, one of *those* things. Like having a tooth out, you mean? Miss Bell always says it's best to take a deep breath and get it over and done with as soon as possible.'

'Miss Bell is very wise,' said Angela.

'Well, it's easy for her to say if she's not the one having the tooth out,' said Barbara. 'But I think she's right all the same.'

And so Angela took a deep breath and returned to the case.

CHAPTER TWENTY

A NGELA'S FIRST STEP was to write a note to Mr. Gil-verson in which she explained with as much dignity as she could muster that, having considered the matter, she believed she had acted too hastily in withdrawing from the case, and that she was willing to devote a little more time to it if he liked. She received by return a letter from the solicitor expressing his gratitude for her patience and his promise that if she did not discover anything new in the next week or two then she should hear from him no more. That done, Angela then summoned Freddy, who accepted the news that she had returned to the case with mixed resignation and enthusiasm, for if he was concerned for his friend he also hated to leave a job half finished, and after all, the case had not been solved yet.

'Have you spoken to the police about the death of Henry Lacey?' asked Angela.

'Yes, but there's nothing much doing,' he replied. 'They knew from Oliver Harrington that he had a visitor on the day of his death but never succeeded in finding out who it was. I don't suppose they tried too hard, since Henry's morphine habit was well known so his death was hardly suspicious. I wonder how Godfrey got him to take the drug. I imagine even someone as far gone as Henry Lacey would notice if somebody stuck a needle in him without permission.'

'Then you're working on the assumption that it was Godfrey who did it?' said Angela.

'Of course. Aren't you?'

'I suppose so,' said Angela, thinking again of Victorine's hands. If those hands were capable of strangling a slightly-built girl, might they also be capable of holding down a man who was under the influence of drink or drugs and forcibly administering an overdose of morphine?

'You seem in some doubt,' observed Freddy. 'But surely his motive is enough to convince you?'

'Oh, yes, that's convincing enough,' said Angela. 'I'm just trying to picture him as a murderer, that's all. He's cold, and while I can quite see him knowing his brother was innocent and letting him hang all the same, I don't know whether he'd be the sort to strangle a woman in a passion. He simply doesn't seem angry enough.'

'I see what you mean,' said Freddy. 'Still, he's our most likely suspect, I should say.'

'What about Oliver Harrington?' said Angela. 'How did he strike you?'

'He didn't seem to have any motive that I could see,' said Freddy. 'And in any case, he says he spent the evening playing billiards with Henry Lacey.'

'Who rather conveniently died and now can't confirm Harrington's alibi one way or the other,' said Angela.

'What, do you think Harrington put Henry out of the way because he knew Harrington was guilty?' said Freddy.

'It's possible, don't you think?' said Angela.

They both considered the idea.

'I can't see it, myself,' said Freddy at last.

'Nor can I, really,' said Angela. 'It's just that I think we oughtn't to fasten upon one suspect at the expense of all the others, since then we might miss something important. If we discount the police's theory that Selina was killed between seven and twenty-five past, then anybody who was in the house at the time might have done it.'

'Any of the men, you mean. Oh, of course, you suspect Victorine too, don't you?'

'Perhaps it is a little far-fetched,' admitted Angela. 'At any rate, I certainly don't suspect Evelyn de Lisle. But if we're looking at likely suspects, then what do you think of Roger de Lisle? I should say that of all the people in the house, he was the one with the personality and temperament to have killed Selina and then put the blame on his son out of spite.'

'Yes,' said Freddy reflectively. 'I hadn't thought of it before, but of course you're perfectly right. It certainly seems to fit everything we've heard about him so far.'

'I hadn't paid much attention to him up to now simply because it seemed unthinkable that he would kill his son's wife and let his son hang for it,' said Angela. 'But of course I was thinking of him as an ordinary person, which he most certainly wasn't. What might seem to you or me to be a ridiculous reason for doing such a thing might have been perfectly logical to his way of thinking. He appears to have been driven into a rage by the slightest thing.'

'You mean Selina accidentally tripped him up in the hall one day and it threw him into such a fury he killed her?' said Freddy.

'Well, perhaps not *quite* such a slight motive as that,' said Angela. 'But there's no saying that she mayn't have offended him in some way, and we know he took offence terribly easily.'

'Do you suppose he was in love with her?' said Freddy.

Angela nodded.

'That's rather what I was wondering,' she said. 'Victorine said that she had the men of the house dancing to her tune. What if one of them was Roger? She said he found Selina charming, and allowed her to take liberties that were not permitted from anybody else. Remember, Oliver Harrington said that it was Roger who first met Selina and brought her to Greystone—and was perhaps even responsible for the engagement between her and Godfrey. I couldn't understand why he was so keen to have her in the family since she had no money, but what if he had become infatuated with her? So infatuated, in fact, that he was willing to allow her to marry his son in order to keep her near him? It's all speculation, of course, but it fits the story as we know it.'

'You think Roger and Selina were having an affair, then?'

'Perhaps,' said Angela. 'It looks pretty certain that Roger had at least one mistress, at any rate. And if one, then why not two?'

'I say, though, it's hardly the decent thing to do, is it? Seduce one's son's wife, I mean. Did Valencourt know about it, do you think?'

I don't know,' said Angela. She felt a pang of something, and to her surprise realized it was sympathy for Edgar Valencourt. Angry as she was at him, she would not wish an unfaithful wife upon him. It was obvious he had been very much in love with Selina, and such a double betrayal by both his wife and his father would have been punishment indeed. 'We don't know for sure how things were. Perhaps Roger was in love with her but it wasn't reciprocated. From what we know of Roger, who evidently liked to have his own way, that might have been enough to make him angry enough to kill her.'

'Still, it seems rather harsh that he should allow his son to take the blame purely because he didn't want to go into the family business,' observed Freddy.

'It does, doesn't it?' said Angela. 'I can't help wondering whether there's something we still don't know. It's just a pity the only people who can tell us the answers are all dead.'

Freddy suppressed a guilty cough and then was struck by a sudden idea.

'I say,' he said. 'Didn't Roger die unexpectedly? A gastric attack, the housekeeper said. What if he was murdered too? I must say that of all the people I should have thought were likely to have been given a helping hand to the next world by exasperated relations, he's the one who springs most obviously to mind.'

'That's true enough,' said Angela. 'But in that case, the murder victims seem to be piling up at an alarming rate. First Selina, then Henry and now Roger. Not to mention Evelyn, who died shortly after the trial, although I can't see why anybody should have had a reason to kill her. Do you really think someone has been doing away with the de Lisle family one by one? It seems a little unlikely.'

'I expect you're right,' said Freddy. 'Still, if it's true it brings us back to Godfrey and Victorine, who are the only ones left. All right, then, let's stick with what we know for certain—which is that Selina's was not a natural death. It seems we have three or four extra suspects to consider now, any of whom might have done the deed after dinner. What do we do now?'

'I told Mr. Gilverson it was useless to try and talk to all the servants who were in the house at the time,' said Angela, 'but as a matter of fact that's not true. I'd really like to speak to the servant who spoke to Selina at a quarter past six. Who was she? Did Selina have a lady's maid?'

Freddy took out his notebook and consulted it.

'I don't recall one being mentioned,' he said. 'In fact, if you remember, Evelyn de Lisle sent her own maid up earlier in the afternoon to see if Selina wanted anything, so I think we may assume she didn't.'

'Then who came to report that she was unwell and would not be coming down to dinner? Surely since whoever it was must have been the last person to see Selina alive, the police ought to have taken her name?'

'One would think so,' said Freddy, squinting at his own hand-writing. 'Perhaps it was the one who ran away.'

Angela glanced up, and an impatient look crossed her face. 'What is it?' said Freddy.

'Oh, nothing. I thought I'd remembered something, that's all, but it's gone now. I have evidently reached the age at which one's mental faculties begin to decline,' said Angela.

'Perhaps you ought to take a holiday after all this,' said Freddy. 'I'm sure it will do you good.'

'So people keep telling me,' said Angela. 'But I seem to have spent most of this year gallivanting and it hasn't helped so far, so I should rather say that a spell of hard work would be more to the purpose.'

'What a ghastly thought,' said Freddy. 'If they required any real work of me at the *Clarion* I should hand in my notice on the spot.' He looked at his watch. 'And speaking of that organ of truth and righteousness, I promised the home editor I'd give him eight hundred words on the accident at the soap factory in Clapham by four o'clock, so I had better go and make a start. Such a pity so many people died, as it means I shall have to resist the urge to pun.'

He took his leave and went out, and Angela was left to think, although with little result, since all her ideas were mere speculation. At length she decided to abandon thoughts of the case for the present. There was an exhibition at an art gallery she wished to see, and she called William to bring the Bentley round to Mount Street. But whether the paintings were uninspiring or whether she was in the wrong frame of mind, somehow she could not concentrate on the matter at hand, and after less than an hour she left.

'William,' she said idly as they returned home, 'I don't suppose you remember the name of the servant who ran away from Greystone Chase, do you?'

William thought.

'Jemima, I think, ma'am,' he said. 'They said she jumped out of a window, but I expect that wasn't true.'

'These things do get exaggerated,' agreed Angela. 'But someone certainly did run away—I know it happened because the housekeeper told me, and she was there at the time. I shall have to ask Freddy to ask the Kent police for her surname. I don't much fancy trying to find her after all this time, but apart from this Mme. Charbonnet—who I doubt will know anything—I have run out of people to question.'

'Winkworth,' said William suddenly.

'What?'

'Jemima Winkworth,' he said. 'That was her name. I've just remembered.'

'Oh,' said Angela. 'Winkworth. Now where have I heard that name recently? Ah, yes. The Misses Winkworth. The woman in the wheel-chair and her sister. Oh!' she said suddenly. 'The elder one called her sister Jemmy, I'm sure of it. I wonder whether it's the same woman.'

She thought back to the day on which she had met the Misses Winkworth on the cliff path. What had the elder one said? Something about them all being dead now, so there was no harm in bringing Jemmy back to Denborough. Who was dead? Was she referring to the de Lisles? Jemmy had been simple in the head, and had had a stroke, and wanted to return to Denborough to die in an expensive nursing-home—far too expensive, in fact, for a woman of her class. Angela stared out of the window and thought very hard.

As soon as they got back to Mount Street she made a tele-phone-call to Freddy. He answered somewhat grumpily, as he was struggling with his piece on the soap factory disaster.

'Listen,' said Angela. 'I think I've found the servant who was the last person to see Selina alive. She's in Denborough and she's quite ga-ga, unfortunately, but I think she knows some-thing and was paid to keep quiet.'

'What?' said Freddy, all thoughts of soap forgotten. 'Who is she?'

Angela explained.

'Yes, I remember them,' he said. 'Those old cats from the Regent were terribly sniffy about it.'

'You have to admit it's a little odd, though,' said Angela. 'I mean, that they can afford that nursing-home. The elder one said that Jemmy had been seen by several doctors, which must have cost a lot of money. What if she saw something and was spirited out of the house afterwards by the de Lisles, who paid her a handsome sum in return for her silence?'

'That's rather a big conclusion you've jumped to,' said Freddy. 'I won't say you're wrong, as it's certainly plausible, but it's not a lot of use to us if her mind's gone, is it?'

'No,' admitted Angela. 'Perhaps her sister can tell us some-thing, then.'

'If Jemmy received money to keep quiet then they're hardly going to talk to us.' said Freddy.

'Then what can we do?' said Angela.

Freddy thought.

'Listen,' he said. 'Let's assume you're right—Jemmy saw something that night, and was paid to leave Greystone and keep her silence. In that case there must surely be a written agreement of some kind, don't you think? If I were the sort to go around carelessly strangling family members in front of the servants and I wanted to buy their silence, I'd probably arrange a nice, fat pension rather than paying a lump sum, which might look suspicious if anybody thought to inquire into the matter. What's the betting there's a letter somewhere which sets out the conditions of the payment?'

'That makes sense,' said Angela. 'But how can we get hold of it?'

'If Jemmy has a copy, which I imagine she does, then it seems to me there are two possible ways to get hold of it: one, charm, and two, burglary,' said Freddy.

'Well, the first one sounds much easier,' said Angela. 'Could you manage that, do you think? You could think up some story and get into Jemmy's room at the nursing-home somehow. If she doesn't have any documents there, at least we might find out the address where they're held. Or failing that, find out where her sister lives. We might try her if we have no luck with Jemmy.'

'Nothing simpler,' said Freddy. 'My charm is legendary. Just say when you want me and I'll be there. Not this afternoon, though, if you don't mind. This piece is determined to defeat me and I'm equally determined it shan't.'

'I have to speak to this Mme. Charbonnet,' said Angela. 'Perhaps I'll do that before we start trying any tricky stuff. In the meantime you might call your sergeant in the Kent police and make quite certain that this Jemmy is the same Jemima

Winkworth we're looking for. It wouldn't do to go bothering a sick woman if she's not the person we're after.'

She promised to let him know when he was needed and hung up. Freddy went back to work and handed in his piece with about a minute to spare, and with only two accidental puns requiring subsequent removal by the editor.

CHAPTER TWENTY-ONE

THE NEXT DAY Angela returned to the Regent Hotel with the aim of finding Mme. Charbonnet. Denborough was a small place, and despite what Marthe had said, Angela did not suppose it to be absolutely teeming with French people, so she did not expect to encounter much difficulty in finding the woman, if indeed she were still living there. Her inquiries at the hotel drew no result, and her first thought after that was to ask Colonel Dempster, but alas, it appeared that he had gone to visit his brother in Cheltenham and would not be back until the next day. Mrs. Hudd had returned in great state to Staffordshire, her two weeks of Kentish festivity behind her for another year, so there was no information to be had from that quarter. Miss Atkinson remained, however, and welcomed Angela with pleasure and some puzzlement, since all this coming and going by Mrs. Wells seemed to her an odd way to conduct a holiday. If she was curious as to why Angela was so particularly interested in the French residents of Denborough she hid it politely, but in any case was unable to help—although she had noticed that there was a servant in the town who seemed to be foreign, to judge by her dress. Angela guessed she was referring to Florence, and decided to turn the matter over to Marthe, who sallied forth into Denborough and was soon able to report to her mistress that Mme. Charbonnet was still living in the town, but had married and was now called Mrs. Poynter.

'Oh!' said Angela. 'Of course! I know her perfectly well. I saw her several times when I was here last. I wonder it didn't occur to me straightaway. She doesn't look at all English. Did Florence say anything about why her mistress came here in the first place?'

'No,' said Marthe.

'Well, that's only to be expected, I suppose,' said Angela. She fell silent, wondering how best to approach the woman, who was presumably living a respectable life these days. It would hardly be good manners to introduce herself and announce that she knew Mrs. Poynter's past history as the mistress of Roger de Lisle—but how else could she question her?

'You'd better give me the address,' she said. 'I don't know whether I've quite the courage to knock on her door, but perhaps I might bump into her when she goes out or in.'

Just then she happened to catch sight of Marthe's face, and saw on it again the worried expression she had noticed so often lately.

'I do wish you'd stop looking at me like that,' she said impatiently. 'It's getting to be rather a bore.'

'*Pardon, madame,*' said Marthe, and busied herself with Angela's things. Angela felt a little irritation.

'Don't try and get around me by putting on that respectful air either, because I know it's all pretence,' she said.

'Excuse me, *madame*, but which is it? Am I to show you my real feelings, or am I to hide them? I cannot do both at the same time.'

'And don't be impertinent,' said Angela.

Faced with such contradictory instructions, Marthe could do nothing but fall silent. There was a pause.

'Look here,' said Angela at last. 'I won't say I'm having fun, because of course I'm not, but you must see why I have to do it. It will all be over soon anyway, and then we can forget about the whole thing.'

'I understand, *madame*,' said Marthe.

'We'll go to New York and see to the business there, and then you shall choose somewhere for us to go if you like, but you must promise to stop fussing.'

'Very well, *madame*, I shall do my best,' said Marthe.

'Good,' said Angela, and went out, leaving Marthe to shake her head in private.

Mrs. Poynter lived in a large, modern brick house on the outskirts of Denborough, in the opposite direction from Greystone Chase. It was not to be supposed that this was the same house in which she had been kept by Roger de Lisle as Mme. Charbonnet, so presumably she had moved here after her marriage. Angela wondered whether Mr. Poynter knew of his wife's past. Colonel Dempster had said there was gossip in the town about her, so perhaps he knew and did not care.

It had begun to drizzle when Angela arrived, and the house was not situated in the sort of area through which one might pass accidentally while out walking, so despite her assertion that she would not knock at the door, Angela plucked up her courage and did so. It was answered by a woman she guessed to be Florence, who informed her that the lady of the house was not at home. Angela turned away and was halfway down the garden path when she spied Mrs. Poynter herself approaching along the cliff top with her little dog. The other woman saw her at the same time and paused for a moment. There was no sense in giving up now, so Angela went boldly up to her and said:

'I beg your pardon, Mrs. Poynter, but might I speak to you for a minute? It's about the murder at Greystone Chase.'

Mrs. Poynter regarded her for a moment. Her expression was wary, but it also held a note of curiosity.

'You are Mrs. Wells, I think,' she said. 'I have seen you before. They say you have been asking questions, but I couldn't quite understand why. Someone said they thought you were a newspaper reporter. Is that true?'

Her accent was quite pure, and apart from a slight rolling of the r, it was almost impossible to tell from her speech that she was anything but English.

'No, I'm not a reporter,' said Angela. 'I'm a sort of detective, and I'm looking into the murder of Selina de Lisle. I understand you were connected with the de Lisle family many years ago, and I wondered whether you might be able to tell me something about what happened at the time.'

Mrs. Poynter gave a short laugh.

'*Connected* with the de Lisles,' she repeated. 'Is that the word they use in Denborough nowadays?' Angela said nothing, and Mrs. Poynter went on, 'I'm afraid you will have to excuse me. I no longer have any *connection* with the family, nor have I for many years. That is a part of my life which is long past, and I have no wish to return to it. True, the old ladies of Denborough like to wag their tongues, but they will have their amusement. I in turn greet them cheerfully in the street, and help them carry their shopping, and run after them if they drop their scarves, and so they have no choice in charity but to tell one another that I am kind-hearted enough for all they know to my disadvantage.'

'But shouldn't you like to see justice done?' said Angela.

'I thought it had been,' said Mrs. Poynter.

'No, it wasn't,' said Angela, and for the first time found she truly believed it. 'They got the wrong man. I want to find out who really did it.'

Mrs. Poynter hesitated.

'What use can it be after all this time?' she said. 'He's dead now, I understand. He has no reputation to lose, whereas I—I have spent more than ten years pretending not to notice when people talk about me behind their hands and forget to include me in invitations. Were it not for the fact that I am as stubborn as a donkey and have determined to see it out I should have persuaded my husband to leave long ago. I dare say you have no idea what it's like to feel the stares of people every time you leave the house, but I can assure you that the last thing I want is to resurrect it all again, just as everybody had begun to forget.'

She nodded and prepared to walk on, but Angela said quickly:

'Oh, but I do. I know exactly what it's like.'

'What do you mean?'

Angela was already regretting her outburst, but there was no sense in going back now. It was time for the truth.

'My real name's not Wells at all,' she said. 'It's Angela March-mont. If you've been reading the newspapers lately I dare say you'll have heard of me.'

'But of course,' said Mrs. Poynter in surprise. 'You were put on trial for the murder of your husband.'

'Yes. I didn't do it, but I was only acquitted because Edgar de Lisle took the blame,' said Angela. She hesitated. 'He didn't kill my husband either, though. He confessed to it to save me.'

Mrs. Poynter regarded her with increased interest. Angela held her chin up proudly.

'I think I see,' said Mrs. Poynter at last. A look of what might have been sympathy appeared on her face. 'Perhaps you had better come in.'

She turned and led the way into the house. Angela followed, her heart beating fast. She had as good as admitted everything to a perfect stranger. Had it been a terrible mistake? But Mrs. Poynter would surely not have invited her in had she not done so.

The house was furnished tastefully in the English style, although here and there were little touches which indicated a foreign hand at work. Mrs. Poynter invited Angela to sit and called for Florence to bring tea.

'You see I have adopted all the English customs,' she said with a smile.

'Do you like living in England?' said Angela.

The other shrugged.

'There was nothing for me in France,' she said. 'My first husband died in the war, and I had no family or money. What else could I do but take what opportunity was offered me? I should have died of hunger otherwise. It was lucky for me that I had my looks. Many other women in my position were not so fortunate.'

'But you might have returned after the war.'

'I might, but my home was destroyed and besides, I was comfortable here. And then I met my husband, who is the kindest and most understanding of men, and that was that. I am not stupid enough to throw good fortune away when it presents itself. And so you think I can help you prove Edgar's innocence?' she went on. 'I am afraid you will be disappointed, for as you can imagine, I was not invited to Greystone very frequently. Roger found me a pretty little cottage and there I was very happy for a while.'

It was the first time Angela had ever heard the word happiness in connection with the de Lisle family, and it sounded odd to her.

'Were you in love with Roger?' she found herself asking.

Mrs. Poynter shook her head.

'Not exactly,' she said. 'He was in love with me, and that was enough for me in those days. I had lost my husband, whom I adored, and I knew I should never love again, but Roger flattered me, and gave me gifts, and told me his troubles, and I felt myself to be a lucky woman when so many others had to dig in the mud just to survive.'

'I had heard that Roger was a difficult man,' said Angela carefully.

'He was,' said Mrs. Poynter. 'He was capricious and jealous, and easily driven to anger, but I knew how to soothe him, which nobody in his family did—least of all his wife.'

'Did she know about you?'

'I imagine so. But one didn't mention such things, of course. We would smile and nod if we saw one another in the street— it would have looked strange not to do so, since we had been acquaintances in France—but it went no further than that. Roger relied on my discretion, and I certainly did not want to cause any upset. Anyway, he told me she did not care. Theirs was not a happy marriage, he said, and it was only right that he look elsewhere if his life at home was less than satisfactory.'

'I don't suppose that courtesy extended to his wife,' Angela could not help saying.

Mrs. Poynter laughed shortly.

'Of course not,' she said. 'We women are not so fortunate in that respect. Society does not afford us the same licence, and Roger certainly would not have allowed such a thing. He used to fly into a rage if he heard of me even speaking to another man, and I expect he was the same with Evelyn.'

'Did you feel sorry for her?' said Angela.

'Perhaps a little,' said Mrs. Poynter. 'I was fond of Roger but, as you say, he was a difficult man. Still, perhaps I was more sorry for his sons. Godfrey in particular had very little freedom. Every part of his life was laid out before him. He was to go to this college, and go into that business, and marry such a woman. He was never allowed to decide for himself.'

'What, he was even told whom to marry?' said Angela. 'Do you mean Roger chose Victorine for him?'

'No, he chose Selina,' said Mrs. Poynter. 'You know, of course, that Selina was engaged to Godfrey first?'

'I had heard it, yes,' said Angela. 'Why was he so keen to have them marry?'

Mrs. Poynter did not answer at first.

'It was a blow to my pride, of course,' she said at length. 'But there is no use in struggling against these things. There comes a time when a man tires of a woman; it is inevitable, I suppose, and Selina was much younger and prettier than I.'

'Roger was in love with her,' said Angela. So her supposition had been correct.

'Yes,' said Mrs. Poynter. 'As soon as he met her his affection for me began to cool—I could see it. He came to me as much as ever, but I could see that he was becoming distant and abstracted, and was not thinking about me. Of course, I had no power, no money of my own, and so I could do nothing about it. I was forced to stand by and watch, knowing that sooner or later I would be cast aside. In the end he even began to confide in me about her. Those were dark times for me, since I had no idea what I should do or where I should go without Roger's protection.'

'Then he brought her into the family with the intention of making her his mistress?' said Angela. 'If that is the case, then

I don't suppose he cared which of his sons married her, as long as one of them did.'

'That is true,' said Mrs. Poynter. 'Still, she was cleverer than he and knew where her power lay. I don't believe she cared a fig for him, but she was poor, and marrying into the de Lisle family would bring her wealth and standing that she should not have had otherwise. Once she was Edgar's wife she led Roger a merry dance, and he soon found out that here was someone who would not bow to his will.'

'Do you mean there was no affair between them?' said Angela.

'Yes,' said Mrs. Poynter. 'He was determined to have her, but she refused him continually. He was driven almost mad, but she knew just how far she could go without compromising herself. She knew that if she gave in to him then all her power would be lost. As I said, she was clever.'

'Do you think her marriage to Edgar was genuine, then?'

'Oh, yes,' said Mrs. Poynter. 'She was in love with him, I'm certain of it. She must have been, or else why should she have risked offending Roger and losing everything she stood to gain by throwing away one perfectly good brother in favour of the other?'

'Did Edgar know about Roger?'

'I dare say he did. I imagine the whole family were aware of it. Roger was not one to hide his feelings, you see.'

'Roger must have been very angry when he failed to win over Selina,' observed Angela.

'Yes,' said Mrs. Poynter. 'He was, even as his love for her grew. Much of the time he was like a bear with a sore head, and I had much ado to calm him. But one day he came to me in a mood which frightened me. I was not afraid of his rages, but this was something different—something cold and ruthless. He would not tell me exactly what had happened, only that he had been betrayed and made a fool of. It had been there under his nose for years, he said, and he would find a way to make them both suffer for it.'

'Goodness!' said Angela. 'Have you any idea what he was referring to?'

'No. He said nothing more, then went away, and the next time I saw him he was his usual self.'

'When was this?' said Angela.

'It was a few weeks before Selina died,' said Mrs. Poynter.

Angela regarded her questioningly. For the first time the other woman seemed uncomfortable.

'You want to know whether I think Roger did it?' she said. 'I do not know. I won't say the idea didn't cross my mind at the time, but I pushed it away. The police were certain it was Edgar, and I had no particular reason to disbelieve it.' She looked Angela steadily in the eye. 'I know nothing for certain, you understand. As far as I knew, Edgar was guilty. Had I believed him to be innocent I should have spoken up at the time.'

'Of course,' said Angela. She was thinking of what had been said. What a strange family the de Lisles had been! For Roger de Lisle to arrange a marriage between his son and the girl with whom he had developed an infatuation, purely in order to keep her close by him, was extraordinary behaviour indeed! And yet Selina had seemed to relish her situation—to revel in it, almost. It now struck her that this must have been what had first attracted Edgar Valencourt to Selina Lacey. Aside from her beauty she had evidently shared his love of danger and his willingness to defy convention. They must have made a wicked pair, the two of them. Had they laughed together at the knowledge that here, at least, was one sure way to thwart Roger? Roger, who had ruled over the household for so many years and cowed his dependants into weary submission, and who was now in thrall to an eighteen-year-old girl? Had Valencourt enjoyed the sight of Roger's frustration when Selina refused to bend to his will? It would hardly have been surprising if he had. But it had turned out to be a deadly game for both of them in the end. Selina had died, and her husband had become an outlaw, driven defiantly into a life of crime and condemned to remain in hiding for the rest of his life.

Angela was now almost certain that here was their murderer. Godfrey had been cast aside by Selina, yes, but with such a life he must have been accustomed to disappointment, and while he might have harboured bad feelings towards his brother, Angela could not picture him committing such a terrible crime and allowing Edgar to hang for it. But Roger—Roger was a different prospect altogether. What could be more likely than that Selina had tested his patience once too often, and that he had finally strangled her and put the blame upon his son—his son, who had defied him, and who had won the prize which had eluded Roger for so long? It all made perfect sense.

But they were still as far away from finding proof as ever. Their one hope now lay in a dying woman named Jemima Winkworth, who could not even speak to them. Had she seen something that night? It must have been something damning, if so. But in that case, why had she allowed herself to be paid off? Somehow they must get into her room and search her things, for without that there was no hope that Edgar Valencourt would ever be exonerated.

Angela stood up.

'Thank you,' she said. 'You've been most helpful.'

'You think Roger did it?' said Mrs. Poynter.

'Yes, I'm afraid I do.'

Mrs. Poynter looked at the floor.

'I shall be sorry if that is the case,' she said. 'But he is dead too, now, so I have not harmed him, at any rate. I was fond of him for a time, and he was always kind to me.' She held out her hand to Angela. 'I wish you success,' she said. 'It will not bring Edgar back, but perhaps you will find some kind of peace.'

'Thank you,' said Angela, slightly taken aback. The thought of having been read so easily made her uncomfortable, and so she took her leave quickly. The visit to Mrs. Poynter had revealed much that Angela had only suspected before, and it all led to the inescapable conclusion that Roger de Lisle had murdered his daughter-in-law and allowed his son to take the blame. Now all that remained was to prove it.

CHAPTER TWENTY-TWO

FREDDY ANSWERED ANGELA'S summons with alacrity, and the very next day he and William came down to Denborough in the Bentley, ready for action. The police sergeant in Kent had confirmed that there had been a housemaid by the name of Jemima Winkworth at Greystone Chase at the time of the murder, and so it seemed as though they had found the person they were looking for.

'I went out this morning in search of the Misses Winkworth,' said Angela. 'I was hoping I might be able to worm some information out of them by means of charm and low cunning, but I didn't see them, which struck me as odd, since they always go out at the same time each day. However, I did see Colonel Dempster, who says the elder Miss Winkworth is unwell with a nasty cold, and has taken herself off home to recover rather than pass it on to her sister.'

'Where does she live?' said Freddy.

'Poplar, apparently. She sent the colonel a postcard, asking if he'd mind paying Jemmy a visit or two to keep her company, until she was well enough to return. He's a kind-hearted soul and agreed.'

'That might make it all the easier for us,' said Freddy, thinking. 'The elder sister's absence, I mean. Have you been to look at the nursing-home in question?'

'Yes,' said Angela. 'It's called The Larches, and it's on one of those wide streets towards the edge of town, a little way past the colonel's cottage.'

'I believe I've seen it,' said Freddy. 'Didn't we pass the gates when we were out walking with those two old dears? Rather a splendid building, all white and gleaming and painful on the eyes when the sun is high. Well-tended lawns and all that.'

'That's the one,' said Angela. 'I paid them a short visit this morning, and told them I was thinking of giving them my elderly mother to look after for a spell, and could they give me a tour? They were only too happy, and so I got a good look at the place. It's very smart and expensive, and they pride themselves on their discretion, so we can't just go wandering about. I'm wondering how to find Jemima's room, though. I'd hoped that since she can't walk by herself but has to use a wheel-chair, she'd be on the ground floor, but the building has lifts, and in any case the director who showed me round told me proudly that the bedrooms are all on the upper floors and have either a sea view or a garden view.'

'Do they have names on the doors?' said Freddy.

'Yes, they do,' said Angela after a moment's thought. 'That ought to make it all the easier if we can get in there.'

'Hmm,' said Freddy. 'Do you suppose we can get a closer look at the place without being accused of loitering?'

'We can if we go in the car,' said Angela. 'Nobody in a Bentley could possibly be suspected of anything but the most honourable motives. And William is bound to be very useful.'

Ten minutes later, the Bentley was parked discreetly in a quiet lane that ran behind The Larches nursing-home. The grounds were bounded by a six-foot wall, and the building itself was only a few feet beyond it. There was no-one about. The three of them stood and stared at the building and debated what to do next.

'I can't ask for another tour of the place,' said Angela, 'but I can distract someone with spurious and idiotic questions if needs be. Although, on second thoughts, perhaps you'd do it better than I should, Freddy.'

'Oh, if it's idiotic questions you want, I'm your man,' said Freddy. 'I shall tell them I'm suffering from dropsy of the elbow and ask them whether it's possible to change rooms every day, since a fortune-teller once told me the only way to cure it is to make sure one's facing North on Wednesdays and South on Fridays. Too fanciful, do you think?'

'Perhaps just a little,' said Angela. 'Unless you *want* them to put you in a strait-jacket and admit you forcibly, of course.'

Meanwhile, William was gazing thoughtfully at the apple trees beyond the wall.

'What do you think, William?' said Angela. 'You look as though you'd had an idea.'

'That tree branch there isn't much more than a foot away from that upstairs window,' he replied. 'It's just a pity the window's closed, or I reckon I could be up there and inside in a flash.'

'Well, keep it in mind as a means of escape,' said Angela.

'What, for all of us? I can't quite picture you climbing a tree,' said Freddy.

'Oh, I was quite the monkey as a girl,' said Angela. 'But these days I am staid and conventional, and prefer to send other people up trees to do my burglaries for me.'

She stopped as she suddenly remembered the last time she had sent someone up a tree.

'You're smiling,' said Freddy. 'What is it?'

'Nothing,' said Angela. 'I'm just thinking that trees are an awfully handy invention for anyone approaching a building with nefarious intent.'

'Very well, then,' said Freddy. 'We need to find Jemima Winkworth's room, get in and search it, then make good our escape. For that we need a plan, since there's no use in trying it when the room is occupied. Do the patients take their meals in their rooms?'

'I believe they do,' said Angela. 'Some of them, at least. Jemmy isn't at all well and needs to be helped with her food, so I expect *she* takes hers in her room at any rate.'

'Well, then, better not try it at meal-times,' said Freddy. 'Presumably the patients don't stay shut up all day, though. The elder Miss Winkworth takes Jemmy out in the mornings, but what do they do in the afternoons?' He glanced at his watch. 'It's ten to two now. Lunch will be over soon, I expect, and it's a pleasant enough day, so I guess we will soon see them emerging in their wheel-chairs to take a little bit of gentle sun in the grounds.'

'We might if we could *see* into the grounds,' said Angela. 'But one can't see anything much from the front gates, and the rest of the place is surrounded by either walls or thick hedges.'

'Pardon me, ma'am,' said William. He jumped lightly onto the bonnet of the Bentley and peered cautiously over the wall. 'There's nobody about,' he said, and before they could stop him sprang up onto the wall and ran along it, shielded from view by the apple trees at the edge of the grounds. After a little way he stopped and gazed through a gap.

'They're all coming out, right enough,' he said, and jumped back down into the lane.

'Give me a leg up, will you?' said Freddy. 'I want to see if Jemima is among them.'

William obliged, and Freddy, balancing precariously on the wall, peered through the trees.

'I can see her,' he announced. 'Or at least, I can see that purple knitted cap of hers. Yes, she's out in the garden all right. She has a nurse with her.'

He swung himself down and brushed the dirt from his hands.

'Very well,' said Angela. 'Listen, I have a plan. I think William will be the best person to carry out the search, so either you or I, Freddy, must go in through the front gates and talk to the woman at the desk in the entrance-hall. Meanwhile you, William, shall climb over the wall and sneak in through the front door while she is nicely distracted.'

'Why can't he simply come in through the front gate?' said Freddy.

'Because it's easily visible from the front of the building, and they're very careful about keeping an eye on whoever comes in,' said Angela. 'The director told me so. William will have to sign the book if he's seen, and we don't want to leave too many traces of our presence, so I think it's best if nobody sees him at all.'

'All right,' said Freddy, 'but isn't there a side door?'

'Yes, there is, but it leads straight into the public lounge, which was very busy when I saw it,' said Angela. 'There's also a back door into the kitchens, but that's no good either, as there will be far too many people about. The main entrance is quiet by comparison.'

'Jolly good,' said Freddy. 'So, then, one of us keeps the girl at the desk busy until William finishes searching the place, and then we make our escape. You'd better work fast, old pal.'

'I don't suppose it will be difficult to find the right room,' said Angela. 'Not if there are names on the doors. You know what you are to look for, don't you, William?'

'I think so,' said William.

'It's a long shot, but it's the only thing I can think of,' said Angela.

'Shall you or I go in?' said Freddy.

'I think you'll probably do it better,' said Angela, 'although I don't like to funk it myself.'

'You won't be funking it. You can stay here and keep the engine running, ready for when we come running out with the loot, so we can make a quick get-away.'

'We're not robbing the place, Freddy,' said Angela patiently. 'We're searching for evidence.'

'Try telling that to the police,' said Freddy, and headed off, ready to play his part.

CHAPTER TWENTY-THREE

I T WAS COOL and dark in the entrance-hall and, as Angela had said, there were few people about. Only the occasional nurse or doctor passed through on their way to some other part of the building. Behind a desk, facing the door, sat a smartly-dressed young lady who straightened up when Freddy entered and gave him a bright smile.

'Good afternoon, sir,' she said. 'Are you here to see a patient?'

'Not exactly,' said Freddy. 'As a matter of fact, I was rather hoping to talk to you.'

'To me?'

'Yes. I'm a reporter for the *Clarion*—I dare say you've heard of it—and I'm here because someone has told me the most extraordinary story about Zelda Delmonico—you know, the film actress—and I want to know whether it's true.'

'Oh?' said the young woman with a look of polite inquiry.

'Yes,' said Freddy. 'I have it on good authority that she stayed in this very nursing-home recently, because the film studio had found out that—'

He beckoned the woman closer and whispered something in her ear. She jumped, startled.

'Goodness!' she exclaimed.

'Quite,' said Freddy. 'You can see why they might want to have the extra one removed.'

The woman shook her head firmly.

'No,' she said. 'We're not allowed to talk about patients, but I can tell you for certain that we have never had this person here at The Larches.'

'Oh, she'll have stayed here under an assumed name,' said Freddy. 'The studios have people to take care of all that kind of thing. They don't want to be associated with any sort of unpleasantness, you see, and you'd be surprised at the lengths they are prepared to go to for their stars. They might arrange for the surgical correction of an unsightly bald patch which gleams unpleasantly under the lights, for example. Or if one of their actors is inclined to associate with unsuitable company, they can make sure he is seen out and about with a succession of pretty young actresses, so people don't get the wrong idea. As a matter of fact, I heard about *one* particular actress who married a famous actor a few years ago, but carelessly omitted to divorce her first husband before the ceremony. The husband threatened exposure and was invited to a meeting with the head of the studio, who was anxious to keep the whole thing quiet. The chap toddled along, no doubt expecting a nice, fat pay-off—and was *never seen again*. Make of that what you will.

I have my own ideas about what happened, of course, but I can't prove it, so perhaps you'd better not mention it.'

The girl was now staring at Freddy with wide eyes, rapt—which was just what Freddy had intended, for out of the corner of his eye he had seen a figure slip quietly in through the front door while the girl was not looking. William's entrance successfully effected, Freddy settled himself down and prepared to flirt.

William, meanwhile, left the entrance-hall and entered a long, brightly-lit corridor. Here he paused, looking this way and that, wondering which way to go. To his right was a lift and, remembering that the patients' rooms were all upstairs, he hurried towards it. On the door was a notice which declared the conveyance to be out of order, and he looked about him for the stairs. Just then, there was the sound of another lift door opening at the other end of the corridor, and he turned to see a middle-aged woman of forbidding aspect, dressed in a nurse's uniform, heading in his direction. William hurriedly felt in his pocket for a screwdriver and began to tinker with the door of the broken lift. The woman stopped when she saw him.

'Ah, it's you at last,' she said. 'They might have sent someone sooner. We've been waiting nearly a week.'

'Soon have it fixed,' said William shortly, in his best Kentish accent.

'Well, make sure you do,' she said, and went on her way.

As soon as she was out of sight, William pushed open a likely door, found the stairs and hurried up to the first floor. Up here all was quiet. William glanced into one or two rooms whose doors were open, and saw piles of sheets and pillows left ready, presumably for the maids. They would no doubt be starting work here soon. He ran down the corridor, reading the names as he passed. At the end was a window, and he looked out and saw it was the same one he had noticed earlier, close to the branches of the apple tree. He followed the corridor to the right and at last found what he was seeking, for there before him was a door which bore the name 'Miss Winkworth.' Glancing to the right and left, William tried the handle carefully, hoping that the room had been left unlocked in preparation for the maids' visit. To his satisfaction the door opened easily and he slipped into the room, bolting it behind him. He looked around. The room was comfortably though sparsely furnished, with a bed, a little cupboard, a chest of drawers, a table and an armchair. A painting of a vase of flowers hung on the wall, and the curtains were heavy, presumably to prevent too much light from getting in and keeping the patients awake. The bed had not yet been made, so William knew he did not have long in which to find what he wanted. Fortunately, there were not many places in which to hide things. He headed straight for the little chest of drawers and searched through it, but found nothing. He scratched his head. A few things were scattered on the table by the window, and he looked among them, but there was nothing of interest here, either. On top of the cupboard was a trunk. William lifted it down and opened it. Inside were clothes and underthings of middling quality, worn and much mended, but no papers, letters or anything else of the sort. He closed the trunk and was in the act of putting it back on top of the cupboard when there was a knock at the door. William started violently and froze, the trunk held over his head. The knock was repeated, then someone tried the door. He heard an exclamation of impatience, then the sound of footsteps retreating down the corridor. He breathed a sigh of relief and returned the trunk to its rightful place.

Time was now pressing, and he paused to think. Assuming Jemima Winkworth did indeed possess an important document of which she was not allowed to speak, where might she have hidden it? About her person, surely—which was no good for William's purposes. She was ill now, however, and under the care of nurses, who presumably would have discovered it when they undressed her, so that seemed to rule that out— unless she had stopped keeping it about her when she fell ill. William frowned, and opened the cupboard. Inside it were one or two good dresses and a heavy woollen coat. It was the wrong time of year for people to be carrying winter coats around with them, thought William. He took the coat out of the cupboard and looked in the pockets. They were empty. He was about to return it to the cupboard when he had a sudden idea. He laid the coat on the bed and ran his hands over the lining. At the front, just under the right sleeve, he heard something crackle, and his heart leapt. Taking out his penknife, he slit open the lining carefully and removed the thing that was contained inside. It was an envelope, grubby and crumpled, bearing the name of a firm of solicitors in Canterbury. This must be what he had come to find! Quickly, William looked to see if there was anything else inside the coat, but found nothing. He hung it back in the cupboard and glanced around to make sure that he had left everything in order. In her state, it was unlikely that

Jemima would ever notice the letter had gone missing—and even if she did, it was needed by someone else now.

As quietly as possible, William emerged from Miss Winkworth's bedroom and ran back down the stairs. As he emerged into the corridor by the entrance-hall, he saw the stern-looking matron he had spoken to earlier standing in close conference with a man whose work-coat and cloth cap declared him to be the real lift mechanic. The matron saw him at the same moment and her eyes widened. William's heart sank.

'There he is!' she said, and took a step towards him.

As quick as lightning, William turned and ran back up the stairs.

'That's done it,' he thought, as he heard shouts behind him. He ducked into the first empty room he saw and hid behind the open door. After a minute, he heard the sound of the matron's voice and that of a man—presumably the mechanic—as they passed.

'He must have come this way,' said the matron. 'We shall have to begin a search.'

'We'll not get far with just the two of us looking,' said the man. 'Why, he might run off any time he likes. While we're searching one room he can duck out of another and be out of here in a trice.'

'Hardly,' said the matron. 'Miss Longfellow has called for help, and is in the entrance-hall, watching the lift and the stairs to make sure he does not escape that way. We'll find him, don't worry. Now, suppose you start at this end. I shall go and fetch the maids.'

William heard the sound of footsteps retreating, followed shortly by a muttered grumble from the mechanic. At any second he expected the man to come in and find him. Instead, he heard what sounded like a match being struck, followed by the sound of the door to the room across the corridor being opened. After a minute, a familiar smell of tobacco could be detected. William decided to take a chance. He peered round the door. Across the corridor, through the open door to the room opposite, he could just see a pair of feet propped comfortably on a table. Evidently the visiting mechanic did not take the threat of an intruder as seriously as the matron did. There was no time to lose. William slipped out of his hiding-place and ran along to the end of the corridor. If the entrance-hall was under observation there was no use in trying to get out the way he had come in. It would have to be the window.

With a little struggle he lifted the sash and climbed out onto the window-sill. It was a narrow one, and he balanced precariously there for a moment, holding on to the lintel above, then pushed the window shut again with his foot, to disguise the evidence of his escape. He worked himself down into a sitting position and glanced back carefully through the window. The corridor was still deserted, but someone would surely be there in a second. The branch of the apple tree was only a few inches away, but it was too thin to hold his weight at this end. There was nothing for it: he would have to jump. He counted to three under his breath, then launched himself with as much force as he could towards a thicker part of the branch—a risky feat for an ordinary man, but William had had a colourful early life and had once been a performing acrobat and, while he was a little out of practice, it was still an easy enough trick for him. He caught the branch, which bent alarmingly but did not give, and hung there for a moment until he caught his breath. He then worked his way along carefully until he reached a place in which the branch would hold his weight easily, and pulled himself up.

For the moment he was safe, but there were people about and he could not risk dropping to the ground and running out through the gates. He would have to go out over the wall into the lane. He scrambled around the trunk to the other side of the tree and began to wriggle along a branch which extended across the wall, then stopped as he heard voices. In the lane below was Angela, talking to Colonel Dempster, who had evidently been walking his dog and was only too pleased to pass the time of day with the elegant Mrs. Wells. William cursed inwardly, for the branch beneath him was dry and seemed reluctant to hold his weight. He attempted to retreat, but there was a loud cracking noise and the branch gave a little. William froze. Just then, Angela glanced up and saw him. She made no sign, but returned to her conversation with the colonel. William held his breath.

At length it appeared that the colonel was preparing to pass on, for he gave a little bow and turned to depart. William gave a great sigh of relief, and at that very moment the branch snapped, depositing him without ceremony onto the top of the wall and thence into the lane, where he landed with a thud at Angela's feet. Angela winced, and Colonel Dempster turned back and started at the sight of the young man lying winded on the ground.

'What's all this?' he said.

'Are you all right, William?' said Angela in some concern.

'I think so,' he said.

Angela helped him into a sitting position, where he remained for a moment, rubbing his elbow.

'I'm afraid the cat escaped,' she said. 'It seems it didn't need rescuing at all. I'm awfully sorry. I do hope you haven't hurt yourself badly. There was a little cat stuck in the tree,' she explained to Colonel Dempster. 'It looked so dreadfully frightened that I couldn't possibly leave it there, so William very kindly agreed to go up and get it. But then it ran off, and so it was all for nothing, I'm afraid.'

'That was very kind of you,' said the colonel to Angela, ignoring the injured party who had done all the work. 'I didn't know you liked cats.'

'Oh, I adore them,' said Angela. 'Poor William is always having to get them out of trees for me.'

'Splendid, splendid,' said the colonel.

At last they got rid of him and were able to ascertain that no bones had been broken.

'I'm sorry about that,' said Angela. 'He turned up and I couldn't get rid of him. I'm glad you're not really hurt.'

'I've had worse falls,' said William.

'Well, it seems you got in all right. Did you find anything?'

William grinned and produced the letter he had found in the lining of Miss Winkworth's coat. Angela drew in her breath as she saw it.

'Let's go and get Freddy,' she said.

CHAPTER TWENTY-FOUR

FREDDY HAD SEEN that the game was up at the nursing-home and had decided that, all things considered, it was better to withdraw before somebody put two and two together and realized what he had been up to. They found him at the hotel, where he was just about to order tea. Since William was the hero of the hour he was invited to join them, and the three of them sat in a quiet corner of the lounge while Angela examined Jemima Winkworth's letter. The envelope contained three or four sheets of paper, which were grubby and much thumbed. Several of them consisted of typed lists of numbers and calculations.

'A pension, by George!' said Freddy. 'Look, it's just as I said! I always knew my enormous powers of the brain were wasted as a reporter. Why, with my deductive skills I ought to be running Scotland Yard. I shall write to them and tell them so. I expect they'll offer me a job on the spot.'

'Look at this,' said Angela, and held out the letter which had accompanied the enclosure. Freddy read.

'Aforesaid disbursements—tum-te-tum—shall be remitted by the aforementioned etc. etc.—on behalf of Roger Valencourt de Lisle—how they do like to rattle on, these legal fellows.'

'Read to the end,' said Angela.

'"—on condition that the aforementioned Jemima Alice Winkworth shall not, now, or at any time, speak to anyone of her employment with the family of de Lisle of Greystone Chase, Denborough, Kent,"' read Freddy. '"Failure to abide by the conditions of this agreement shall render it null and void, and any monies disbursed theretofore to the said Jemima Alice Winkworth shall be liable to be repaid at a rate of—" goodness, he even threatened to claim the money back with interest if she didn't keep quiet.'

'Yes,' said Angela. 'An inducement and a threat at the same time.'

'Then it *was* Roger de Lisle who did it,' said Freddy. 'But you do realize this still doesn't prove anything, don't you? It looks suspicious enough, given the amount he was paying her, but the police won't be interested without something more solid. And besides, they might reasonably point out that it merely suggests that Jemima saw *Edgar* do it, and that Roger paid her off to protect him, even though his scheme failed in the end.'

'True,' said Angela. 'I think perhaps it's time to go to Poplar and speak to the elder Miss Winkworth. She must know something of all this, surely.'

'She won't speak, though,' said Freddy.

'She'll have to,' said Angela firmly. 'We must get her address off the colonel. What shall we tell him? I know—we'll say we want to send her some flowers, or something.'

Freddy was dispatched in search of Colonel Dempster and Angela insisted on standing William high tea for his trouble. 'After all,' she said, 'I couldn't possibly have done it myself. But thanks to you it rather looks now as though we're on to something. I hope Miss Winkworth won't be too difficult.'

'What if she won't speak?' said William.

'Then I shall have to appeal to her better nature,' said Angela.

The next morning, Angela and Freddy found themselves walking down a street in East London, looking for a particular house. The street was one of the more respectable addresses in Poplar, and it was clear that its residents were relatively well-to-do. At last they arrived at the number they were seeking. Its front door was painted a cheerful red, while the doorstep was as clean as a pin and the brass knocker had been polished until it shone.

'I hope she's in,' said Angela, glancing about as she rapped on the door. 'I've seen a few curtains twitch, and I fear the gossips will be licking their lips at the sight of us. The approval of the neighbours is everything in this sort of place, I understand.'

As she spoke, she saw another curtain twitch in the window by the front door, which was shortly afterwards opened by the elder Miss Winkworth. She was red about the eyes and wheezing a little, but she regarded them in cheery surprise.

'Hallo, hallo, I know you,' she said. 'What brings you all the way to my little house?'

'Miss Winkworth, we'd like to speak to you about your sister,' said Angela.

A look of alarm crossed Miss Winkworth's face.

'She hasn't taken a bad turn, has she?' she said. 'I hope she hasn't caught my cold.'

'No, no, it's nothing like that,' Angela hastened to assure her. 'It's about what happened at Greystone Chase.'

'I don't know what you mean,' said Miss Winkworth warily.

'Your sister was a housemaid there, I believe?' said Freddy.

'Yes, but that was a long time ago,' said Miss Winkworth.

'Eleven years ago, to be precise,' said Freddy. 'Around the time of the murder of Selina de Lisle. We know she saw something and was paid to keep quiet.'

Miss Winkworth had gone pale.

'I still don't know what you're talking about,' she said. 'You've got the wrong person. Good day to you.'

She made to shut the door, but Angela produced the letter they had taken from Jemima's coat.

'We have proof she was paid a pension by Roger de Lisle on condition that she say nothing about what happened,' she said. 'It's in this letter. I can read it to you if you like.'

'Where did you get that?' said Miss Winkworth. 'Did you steal it from her? How did you get hold of it?'

'Never mind how we got hold of it,' said Angela. 'It's important evidence that might clear a man's name and it oughtn't to be kept hidden. Now, are you going to talk to us or not?'

Miss Winkworth seemed to sag a little.

'Have you come to ask for the money back?' she said. 'Because she can't pay it. You know the state she's in.'

'No, that's not why we're here,' said Angela. 'All we want is to know what happened.'

'All right, then, I suppose you'd better come in,' said Miss Winkworth, after a moment's hesitation. 'I was never easy about it, and she's not long for this world so what harm can it do her now?'

They followed her into a dim front parlour, which was evidently kept for best and little used, for the chairs were covered with sheets. Miss Winkworth whisked the covers off hurriedly and invited them to sit. They did so, while she perched awkwardly on another chair and regarded them with something like fear.

'It wasn't her fault,' she said suddenly. 'She was always simple, and she didn't understand what it was she'd seen. Then afterwards when Mr. de Lisle came to her and said he wanted to reward her for all her hard work, she believed him. If she'd spoken to me at the time I'd have told her to go straight to the police, but she didn't tell me about it until long afterwards, and by then it was too late—she'd signed the agreement and couldn't go back on it.'

'What did she see?' said Angela gently.

Miss Winkworth rubbed her hands together in agitation.

'I can show you her letters, if you like,' she said. 'Then you'll understand why she wasn't to blame.'

She rose and went across to a large dresser which was loaded down with knick-knacks, chipped teacups, china dogs, framed photographs and hundreds of other things besides, and opened a drawer. Inside was a pile of letters, and she brought them out and began to rifle through them.

'I ought to have burned them,' she said. 'I knew they'd bring nothing but harm in the end. Here.' She picked out two or three letters from the sheaf and handed them to Angela. They had been written in the autumn of nineteen eighteen, and were addressed in a childish hand to a Miss Maria Winkworth. 'That's me,' said Miss Winkworth helpfully. 'She'd been living in Deal, in a house Mr. de Lisle found for her. He thought she'd like it there, he said. I didn't hear from her for months and I thought she'd disappeared, but she got lonely after a while and wanted someone to confide in, so she wrote to me. Eventually she left Kent and came here to live with me, and we got along well enough until she was taken sick.'

Angela read the first letter, then glanced at Freddy and handed it to him without a word. Jemima's ability to express her ideas was hardly the best, but what she had to say was clear enough. The letter read as follows:

My very dear Maria,

Thank you for your last I am glad you are keeping well and that you found your blue gloves, the weather has been cold here and if Poplar has been anything like it you will be glad of them. I have been thinking about what you said the other day about whether the fortunate position I am in thanks to Mr. Roger de Lisle was quite proper, and there is something I am not easy in my mind about, and I would like to ask your opinion about it. I did not think about it at all then but after what you said I have come to realize there is something not right about what happened. I told you Mr. de Lisle said I must show my loyalty and say nothing to the police about what I had seen if I wanted to receive the money, but truly Maria I had no idea what he meant at the time. But now it seems to me that there must have been something wrong with what I saw even though I had no idea of it then for why should they give me money and send me away if there was nothing wicked in it? They were all so unhappy at the big house that it was nothing to hear snapping and grumbling through a door, and that is why I thought little of it. I kept my head down and minded my own business and kept polishing, and I did not listen to what the man was saying until his voice became so loud I had no choice. He wanted her to do something but she would not, and she was laughing at him. I heard her say he must have been mistaken and that she loved her husband and no-one else, and then she asked him to congratulate her and said how he must be so very happy that he would soon have a grandchild to remind him of his son and carry on the family name. I was listening then because I had not heard that she was with child, and when I passed the door which was open a little way I turned my head just quickly to see if I could see it on her, and there she was with that saucy look as she always wore. I could not see him but I knew from his voice that it was the master. When I came back I saw him, carrying her in his arms. He was very pale and seemed not to know what to do so I stopped and said Oh she has fainted Sir, shall I fetch help? And he said not to worry, but that he would carry her to her room and fetch his wife. He told me to say nothing to Mr. Edgar as Mrs. de Lisle would not wish her husband to know because he would be angry at her for getting up when she was meant to be in bed. Then when she was discovered dead the next day I thought Mr. Edgar must have found out after all and been so furious with her that he had killed her. I believed Mr. Roger de Lisle thought the same because that is when he came to me and said that it was a dreadful affair and that he was afraid Mr. Edgar would be arrested, and for the honour of the family it would be better to say as little about it as possible so as not to make things any worse than they were, then he talked about my hard work and said he was thinking of giving me a handsome pension if I would hold my peace. You know Maria that the work had become hard for me of late, and that the pains in my hands and knees were almost too much to bear, and I did not wish to make things worse for Mr. Edgar who was always very kind, and that is why I agreed to it. It was not as though my silence was of any use to the police since they arrested him anyway so I did not feel I was doing wrong. In any case I had accidentally mentioned her fainting to Mr. Henry Lacey before Mr. de Lisle told me to keep quiet, so he knew about it too and I knew he would know what to do. He was surprised but said that he would speak to Mr. Roger de Lisle about it, but that I should keep quiet about it as I had been told. But now Maria I am wondering whether I have been taken for a fool. It all happened so very quickly that I did not have a minute to think about it carefully.

How I wished for you to advise me but I was hustled and bustled about and told not to say a word if I did not want to make things worse, and then Mr. Roger de Lisle took me to Deal and said it was to be my home, and showed me a cheque for twenty pounds and said I was a good girl and should have it now but that if I wanted more I must sign an agreement and in the meantime I must stay hidden. He came back the next day with the papers, and explained to me what all the words meant, and how much I was to receive every month, and in the end I signed because after all what else could I do? But now I see what you have probably understood immediately yourself but which I did not realize at the time. I think now that I saw Mr. Roger de Lisle with the dead body of Mrs. de Lisle and that he killed her even as I was there outside the door polishing a brass vase and blamed it on his son. I do not know what to do about it, Maria. If he is really so wicked then I am also wicked for I have taken money to keep quiet. What if Mr. Edgar is innocent? I know he has escaped from prison but they will surely find him soon and hang him. I want to go to the police but I am afraid they will not believe me or that they will arrest me. What do you think I ought to do? Please write back and give me advice and if you can, comfort.

Fondest wishes
Jemima

'You see?' said Miss Winkworth as Angela and Freddy glanced at one another again. 'She was all alone and easily taken advantage of. She wasn't to blame, but once she'd signed the agreement and taken the money there was no way out of it for her, and I told her so. The police would have arrested her. An accessory, they call it. She was an accessory, although she didn't know it. We've always been respectable people and it wouldn't have done to have the police on our doorstep.'

Angela glanced through the other letters. Maria Winkworth had evidently asked Jemima for more details about what she had seen, since they contained a more precise description of the events of the day. Roger had killed Selina at about a quarter to six, and had told Jemima to say nothing but to go and report downstairs that Mrs. de Lisle would be spending the evening in bed. Presumably he had then locked Selina's bedroom door and put her body in the cupboard in Valencourt's room. It appeared too that after Selina had been found, Henry Lacey had tried to approach Jemima—presumably since he had by now guessed what had really happened and wanted to know more. However, Roger was keeping a sharp eye on her, and that very evening, while the police were still examining the scene in the wood, he had spirited her away to the house in Deal and told her to stay there until he returned. After she had signed the agreement he warned her that she was now bound by her word, and that if she broke it the police would come and arrest her and she would be thrown into prison for many years for obtaining money under false pretences. Thus was Jemima Winkworth bribed and frightened into keeping silent about the murder she had witnessed—although she had not been able to stop herself from telling all to her sister, who had also kept quiet since she was horrified at the very idea of Jemima's being arrested for complicity in the crime.

'Is this enough, do you think?' said Freddy to Angela after they had read all the letters.

'I hope so,' said Angela. 'If they won't act after they've read all this then they never will. I'm afraid we must take these,' she said to Miss Winkworth. 'They're terribly important and they might just clear Edgar de Lisle's name. I'm sorry for your sister, but you must understand that we can't allow this state of affairs to continue.'

'I suppose not,' said Miss Winkworth. 'I expect the pension will stop now. At least the nursing-home is paid up until the end of the month so they won't throw her out tomorrow. It's a pity, though; she did so want to end her days in Denborough. Now I suppose she'll have to come here.'

'We shall have to see what can be done,' said Angela, who felt obliquely guilty about uprooting a dying woman from her comfortable bed even though her care had been paid for illicitly.

'Will they arrest me?' said Miss Winkworth fearfully. 'After all, I knew about it too.'

'I doubt it,' said Freddy. 'Although they might want to question you, since your sister can't speak for herself.'

'Oh, Jemmy,' said Miss Winkworth sadly. 'What have you done?'

There was no suitable answer to that, so Angela and Freddy took their leave and left.

CHAPTER TWENTY-FIVE

T HEY HAD PROMISED to call in to see the colonel and report on Miss Winkworth's health, so they returned to Denborough one last time.

'One thing I still don't understand is why Roger deliberately put the blame on his son,' said Freddy, as the train chugged over the grimy streets of South London on its way to the Kent coast.

'Perhaps there had been some particular offence,' said Angela. 'I can't believe he did it merely because Valencourt had refused to work for him. I think that would be too much even for Roger. There's no doubt that he strangled Selina out of jealousy, but I don't know about anything else. Perhaps it was because Edgar had got the thing that Roger wanted and could never have. Who knows?'

'So he strangled Selina, then hid her body in the cupboard in order to leave incriminating evidence in Valencourt's room,' said Freddy. 'Then he must have drugged Valencourt to make him sleep soundly, since otherwise it would have been impossible to get her out and take her to the woods.'

'Yes, Valencourt suspected himself that he had been drugged,' said Angela. 'I suppose the removal of the body was just an extra touch by Roger to make his son look even more guilty. Anyone might have hidden Selina in the cupboard, but only Valencourt had a reason to get her *out* of the cupboard, since obviously he wouldn't want her to be found in his room.'

'When do you suppose Roger thought of the plan to incriminate Valencourt?' said Freddy. 'You don't suppose the whole thing was premeditated, do you?'

'No,' said Angela. 'I don't think the murder was planned. Presumably the idea of pinning the blame on his son must have come to him afterwards. It was easy enough to do, after all.'

'Well, it was ill-natured of him, to say the very least,' said Freddy. 'And it does sound rather as though Henry Lacey may have been put out of the way too, since it looks pretty certain he knew what had really happened.'

'We'll never prove that was murder,' said Angela. 'There's no use in even trying. Still, I shall mention it to the police and perhaps they'll look into it again.'

'Rather terrible to think that he was so dependent on the drink and the morphine that he was prepared to keep quiet about his own sister's death in return for the money to support his habits,' said Freddy.

Angela nodded but did not reply. Freddy was jubilant at their success in solving the case and she knew she ought to feel the same, but instead she felt nothing but a bleak emptiness. She had paid off her debt, but at what cost? Now she no longer had any reason to justify the wrong she had done. When, standing in the dock of the Old Bailey, she had denied having ever met Edgar Valencourt in order to save herself, she had done so with his tacit approval—encouragement, even, but then she had been able to find selfish comfort in the thought that, as the murderer of his wife, he deserved everything he got. Now, through her own efforts, she had discovered that it was all a lie; that he was an innocent man—innocent of murder, if not of other things—and because of that the whole edifice of half-truths she had built in her head since January to convince herself that she had not acted wrongly was exposed for what it was: a house of straw which one gust of wind in the form of Jemima Winkworth had now blown away. Her guilt was laid bare and at that moment she knew it would be with her forever.

Freddy glanced at her in surprise at her silence, and was shocked at what he saw, for his friend suddenly looked tired and pale, her brow drawn and her eyes hollow.

'Are you all right, Angela?' he said. 'You look as though you'd had a shock.'

'Yes, I'm quite all right, thank you,' she said. 'We'll go and say goodbye to the colonel and Miss Atkinson, and then I suppose I'd better pay a visit to Scotland Yard. It's about time I told them the truth about everything.'

Freddy regarded her with sympathy.

'You're not really all right, are you, old girl?' he said. 'I mean, you put on a good show and all that, but it's pretty obvious you're unhappy.'

Angela turned to him suddenly.

'Unhappy?' she said bitterly. 'Why should I be unhappy? I'm alive, aren't I? I have my health and my friends; I'm comfortably off; I'm invited to all the most fashionable parties; I'm spoken of as one of the best-dressed women in London. I have every reason to be perfectly content. Of course, I'm having to face the fact that I sent the man I loved to his death for no good reason, but one can't have everything, can one? Leaving that aside, I'm about to hand Scotland Yard the solutions to two crimes, so in addition to everything else I can pique myself on my own cleverness. They might arrest me when I tell them the truth, but let's not worry about that, shall we?'

'Then why tell them?' said Freddy, taken aback. 'Why not keep it to yourself?'

'And add another lie to my account? Thank you, Freddy—I appreciate your concern, but it's time I put things right.'

She refused to say another word on the subject and in fact relapsed into silence for the rest of the journey. By the time they arrived in Denborough she was her usual cheerful self again, as though her earlier outburst had never happened. Freddy was tactful enough not to mention it, but he felt he had seen a side of Angela he had only ever suspected existed, for her cool façade was the result of long practice and she did not let it down lightly. Now he knew for certain that she felt things as deeply as anybody else he could not help but admire the strength of character she had shown over the past few months, for evidently it had taken great effort and was not merely born of an inability to feel.

They found Miss Atkinson about to leave, and Freddy gallantly offered to accompany her to the station with her luggage.

The two of them went off, and Angela found herself assailed by a sudden urge to visit Greystone Chase one last time, for she could not help thinking that it was only fair to warn Godfrey of what was about to happen. After all, the police would surely want to come and question the de Lisles again, and they might, not unreasonably, be curious as to why the whole thing had been stirred up again. How would Godfrey take it, she wondered. Would he be angry? She had no idea as to whether he had liked his father or not.

As she approached the house she stopped to look at it. Solid and imposing as it was, it gave no sign of the unhappiness which had dwelt within its walls for so many years. Soon it would be sold and another family would come to live there, and perhaps erase the bad memories. As she stood there she saw a figure she recognized come out and walk down the path towards the gates. It was Victorine de Lisle. She hesitated briefly when she saw Angela, then changed direction and came towards her.

'You again,' she said in her brusque manner.

'Yes,' said Angela. 'I really came to see your husband.'

'He is in France, and will not be back until next week,' said Victorine.

'That's a pity,' said Angela. 'I had something important to tell him—to tell you both. New evidence has been found which proves that Edgar de Lisle didn't kill his wife after all.'

'Oh?' said Victorine with distant interest. 'Who did it?'

'I think you know,' said Angela.

Victorine raised her eyebrows.

'I suppose now you are going to say it was my father-in-law,' she said.

'Yes. Did you know before?'

'He was in love with her,' said Victorine. 'It was never mentioned, of course. If Edgar did not do it then of course it must have been Roger. Who else could it have been?'

'But why didn't you say something at the time, if you suspected?'

'I did not suspect anything then,' said Victorine. 'Perhaps afterwards, but by then it was too late. And what purpose could it serve to bring it all up again? I had no proof, and we still had to live with him.' She gave a short laugh. 'Do you suppose it would have been good for domestic harmony to have one half of the family accusing the other half of murder? I could do nothing—nor did I wish to.'

'You seem anxious to protect Roger,' said Angela. 'Why?'

'Protect him?' said Victorine. 'Of course I did not want to protect him. He was a wicked, wicked man. He told his own wife he had seen Edgar kill Selina, and he almost convinced her of it. She died of a broken heart. I liked Evelyn, but I hated him more than I have ever hated anyone, especially for how he treated Godfrey—how he treated all of us. We suffered for years from his cruelty until we thought we could no longer bear it. He was a vicious, black-hearted man, who caused nothing but unhappiness.'

'Then why didn't you do something?' said Angela. 'He got away with murder and was never punished.'

'What makes you think he was not punished?' said Victorine.

Angela looked up and saw a glint in her eye.

'Why, because he was never arrested for the murder or even suspected of it,' she said.

'No,' said Victorine. 'But there are other forms of punishment. The devil always comes to claim his own in the end.'

'What do you mean?' said Angela.

'He is dead, no?' said Victorine. 'He died painfully, of food poisoning. At least that is what they say. Godfrey and I were there at the time. He suffered greatly, and then he died.'

She said it carelessly, and there was a smile playing about her lips. Angela regarded her curiously. Was this a confession? It would not have surprised her in the least to discover that Victorine had taken matters into her own hands—those large, strong hands of hers which might have squeezed the life out of a slightly-built girl had she wanted them to. Had they instead administered a lethal dose of something to Roger de Lisle? Victorine held her gaze, still wearing that satisfied smile, and Angela, after a moment's thought, decided not to rise to the challenge. She had had enough of the de Lisles and their intrigues, she realized, and wanted no more of them. Let them all murder each other if they liked; she no longer cared. Victorine might enjoy her triumph—if such it was—in peace. Whether or not it was an empty boast, Angela could not find it in her heart to feel sorry for Roger de Lisle. He had been a wicked man, but his soul was long beyond the reach of mortal man to save.

'I gather food poisoning can be a terrible thing,' she said politely at last.

Victorine nodded in satisfaction.

'I expect there will be a new investigation into Selina's murder,' she said, as though Roger had never been mentioned. 'We shall be here if the police wish to speak to us.'

And with that she turned on her heels and went on her way.

CHAPTER TWENTY-SIX

THE TIME HAD now come to hand over the evidence of Roger de Lisle's guilt to Scotland Yard. Charles Gilverson, who was overjoyed at Angela's success, was only too keen to accompany her, as was Freddy, but she insisted on going alone, for she had an explanation to make which she did not want anybody else to hear. Accordingly, she presented herself and asked to see Inspector Alec Jameson. She had seen little of him in recent months—partly because he was newly married and had other things to do, and partly because her guilty conscience would not allow her to associate freely with those who were supposed to represent the law when she herself had behaved so badly. This made her sad, for she was very fond of Jameson and his wife, but she had judged it better to keep away from them as far as possible in order not to put them in a difficult position.

Jameson himself came out to greet her.

'Now, isn't that odd,' he said when he saw her. 'I was just thinking about you and wondering where you'd been hiding. And now here you are!'

'Yes, here I am,' she replied. 'Do you have a moment? Or perhaps an hour or two might be more to the purpose. I've something rather important to tell you.'

'Why, of course,' he said, surprised at her sober expression. He ushered her into his office and they sat. 'What is it?'

Angela brought out the letters she and Freddy had taken from Jemima and Maria Winkworth.

'A few weeks ago, I was asked to look into a murder which took place eleven years ago, in Kent,' she said. 'A man was arrested and found guilty of the crime, but escaped and was never hanged. He died a few years later, still protesting his innocence. I have now found proof that someone else committed the murder, and I should like you to arrange for the new evidence to be submitted to the Home Office so that the man may be granted a posthumous pardon.'

'Goodness me,' said Jameson. 'I thought you had decided to give up detecting, but it appears you've changed your mind.'

'I haven't changed my mind,' said Angela. 'This was a particular case and I didn't feel I could say no. The man in question is Edgar de Lisle, better known to you as Edgar Valencourt. He didn't murder his wife, and I can prove it.'

Jameson regarded her in astonishment.

'Edgar Valencourt? You mean the man who killed your husband?' he said.

'Yes, well, that's another matter,' said Angela in some confusion. She recovered herself quickly. 'I'll come to that in a

234

moment. Let me tell you about the murder of Selina de Lisle first.'

She did so methodically, starting from the letter she had received from Mr. Gilverson—although she did not mention her letter from Edgar Valencourt—and ending with their visit to Miss Winkworth in Poplar.

'Here are the letters Jemima Winkworth sent to her sister,' she said at last, handing them to Jameson. 'As you can see, it seems rather obvious that she witnessed the murder itself—or near enough, at least. And Roger de Lisle's behaviour in spiriting her out of the house immediately and promising her money in return for her silence certainly seems incriminating to me. I'm not sure whether our methods in obtaining the letter from Jemima in the nursing-home were strictly legal, but I rather think Maria Winkworth will keep quiet about it.'

'Let me look at this before I decide whether to give you a telling-off,' said Jameson. He read the documents quickly, then sat back. 'Well, at first glance it certainly looks as though you might have a case, although I shall have to look into it more carefully—and, of course, I don't make this sort of decision. It will all have to be passed to the powers-that-be first.'

'But you think there's a possibility he might be pardoned?' said Angela eagerly.

'Who knows?' said Jameson. 'These things take months, but I've seen pardons granted on less evidence than this.'

'If it can be proved that Henry Lacey was also murdered, then I think the case against Roger might be strengthened,' said Angela. 'I don't know how that might be done, though.'

'We can certainly look into it,' said Jameson. 'But Angela, why did you agree to investigate this? I should have thought that you, of all people, would be the last person to want to help Edgar Valencourt, the murderer of your husband.'

Angela steeled herself. It was time to tell the whole truth.

'That's just it,' she said. 'He didn't kill Davie.'

'What do you mean?' said Jameson. 'Of course he killed Davie. All the evidence fitted, and he actually confessed to it.'

Angela brought out another document which she had been keeping with her solicitor. It was the signed statement from Callie Vandermeer, who had been a witness to Davie's death.

'You'd better read this,' she said, and handed it to him.

There was silence as the inspector read the document carefully. When he had finished he looked up in surprise.

'What's all this?' he said. 'Who is this woman? This isn't what happened.'

'I'm afraid it is,' said Angela. 'She's in America at present, but she has promised to come and testify to what she saw if needs be. I haven't the slightest doubt that she was telling the truth. Freddy and I found her after I was released and got her to sign this statement. She had the keys to my flat in her possession when we spoke to her.'

'But then why did Valencourt confess to having done it?' said Jameson, who was becoming increasingly perplexed.

Angela looked at her hands.

'I have a confession of my own to make,' she said. 'And I'm afraid you're going to be terribly disappointed in me.' She looked up, took a deep breath, and went on, 'Edgar Valencourt was a—a friend of mine. I lied to the court when I said I'd never met him. I was with him on the night Davie died. I didn't kill Davie—I wasn't even at home that night—but it was obvious they were going to find me guilty, so Edgar came forward and took the blame on my behalf. I should have told you sooner, but he escaped and there didn't seem any sense in it after that. Still, the very least I could do after he saved me was to try and help him in return. Now I have. It's too late for him, of course, because he's dead now, but I won't let it be said he was a murderer when he was nothing of the sort.'

Jameson was staring at her, astounded, and she looked away.

'I know it was wrong of me,' she said. 'Very wrong. But— well, what's done is done. I didn't approve of myself at all, but my intentions were good, at least.' She laughed sadly. 'If you want to know where I was on the night of my husband's death, I was in Faversham, forcing Edgar to return a stolen brooch through a letter-box. Silly, isn't it?'

'I remember that,' said Jameson. 'It had the Kent police scratching their heads for a while. So it was you, was it? I didn't realize Valencourt was part of the Boehler gang.'

'He wasn't,' said Angela. 'He stole the brooch from them and they killed him for it. At any rate, you can see why I didn't have a satisfactory alibi for that night. I was driving around the countryside with a notorious thief and couldn't have proved it even if I'd wanted to.'

'I see,' said Jameson. 'But Angela, lying in court is a very serious matter.'

'I'm perfectly aware of that,' said Angela. 'And you might as well give it its proper name, perjury. I can't even claim I did it for any higher purpose. I lied to save myself. I didn't come here to throw myself on your mercy, Alec. I fully expect to be prosecuted for what I did. But I didn't want to have to tell everything to Inspector Scott or someone equally unsympathetic, and I knew you would be kind, if only for old times' sake.'

The last part was said in a low voice, and it would have taken a much harder man than Alec Jameson to withstand such an appeal.

'Stop looking at me as though you expect to be hit over the head and arrested at any minute,' he said at last. 'I won't deny I'm surprised—and the super won't be any too happy either, since it looks as though we'll have to reopen the investigation into your husband's death, but I'm not going to throw you in prison quite yet.'

'I'm not asking for preferential treatment,' said Angela, who, now she had decided to admit the truth, was determined to be punished for it.

'I'm glad to hear it,' said Jameson. 'Now, listen, Angela. You've given me rather a lot to think about, so I suggest you go home and let me get on with it. If you want to do things properly then I don't mind telling you not to leave London without letting me know, but other than that you're free to go.'

'But—' said Angela.

'I can't tell you what's going to happen, because I don't know,' said Jameson. 'I'll have to speak to the super. As I've said, perjury's a serious matter, but he may decide there were extenuating circumstances, since you'd probably have been hanged for murder had you told the truth.' He shook his head, as though to clear the cobwebs from it. 'I don't think I've ever come across anything like this in all my years as a policeman,' he said. 'Now, you'd better go before I change my mind.'

Angela did as she was bid and went home, feeling slightly deflated, for she had fully expected to be arrested. Jameson, meanwhile, sat at his desk for a good twenty minutes after her departure, staring into space unhappily and wondering what to do.

CHAPTER TWENTY-SEVEN

THERE WAS NO denying that Angela's confession had come as something of a shock to Inspector Jameson. During her trial certain facts had emerged which had revealed a darker side to her character, so it was not as though he had considered her to be a model of virtue. She was not the first woman to have been caught out in that way, and nor would she be the last. However, this latest revelation that she had deliberately allowed herself to be drawn into an illicit entanglement with a criminal and had lied about it before a court was something which was more difficult to understand and forgive. She was a sensible woman—far too sensible to engage in such nonsense, and so it seemed to him that she had done it out of a sort of arrogance, an assumption that her position in society meant that she might do what she liked and nothing could touch her. In fairness, it must be admitted that she had been punished for that arrogance; her public humiliation had been thorough and complete, and yet Jameson was still unhappy at what had been revealed about his old friend, and what it meant for the cases they had worked on together. He had always supposed her to be completely honest, and on that supposition had been happy to accept her help in solving several murders in the last three years. But could she be relied upon? Had any of the cases been compromised by what he now knew about her? As a conscientious policeman he had to admit the possibility that innocent people might have been condemned. He set himself to consider each case one by one, and to his relief came to the conclusion that there were no problems on that head; he himself had been in charge on each occasion and he flattered himself that he had not been taken in. But, then, what was he to think about Angela? And what was he to do about the fact that she had lied in court?

He wrestled with the problem for some while longer, then decided to go home, which lately had become his comfort and his refuge from the cares of his job. His wife Kathie welcomed him with her usual smiles and kisses, and saw immediately that he was troubled by something. She did not ask about it, for she knew that if it were something she was permitted to hear he would tell her about it sooner or later. And he did, for she, too, was a friend of Angela, and indeed had been helped by her in one of their earlier cases—might even have been in prison now had it not been for her. Kathie was certainly surprised by what her husband had to say, but she was less disturbed by the knowledge of Angela's indiscretions than by the fact of her undoubted suffering, for she would not admit for a second that Angela was anything less than the person she had always appeared. As she pointed out, there was no need for Angela to have investigated the de Lisle case at all, and the fact that she had done so, even though she knew that the game would be up for her, proved her to be as honourable as they had always known her to be. As for her association with Edgar Valencourt—why, who had any choice in the matter when it came to falling in love? Alec might remember that not so long ago he had himself fallen for a murder suspect, despite all his best efforts. It had turned out very well for the two of them—but poor Angela had no such comfort to receive, for she was all alone, with nothing ahead of her except the likelihood of another court case and further notoriety.

Jameson looked at his lovely wife and thought of the happiness she had brought him, thanks in part to Angela Marchmont. It was thanks to Angela's curiosity and determination that he could now look forward to the prospect of passing on his name to another generation—he and Kathie had even talked of naming the child Angela if it was a girl. As his wife had said, who was he to pronounce judgment? Angela had done wrong, but she was now doing her best to put things right, and surely the intention was to be applauded. Very well: he would follow Kathie's example and forgive, although that still left the matter of the perjury to be resolved, for he could not keep that to himself, given that it was an essential part of the explanation in not one, but two murder cases.

The next day, therefore, Jameson presented himself before his superintendent with the documents he had been given, and did his best to tell the story so as to present Angela in the best light he could. The super was not a good-tempered man as a rule, and was inclined to take the worst side of things, but as it happened he had a long-standing and immovable dislike of the superintendent of the Kent police, and the idea of putting one over on his deadly rival by proving him to have been wrong in the de Lisle murder put him in a most unaccustomed good mood, and inclined him to look at other matters a little more leniently. Besides, the press had got wind of that case, thanks to Freddy Pilkington-Soames, and dozens of reporters were sniffing around Scotland Yard and writing congratulatory pieces about the return of Angela Marchmont to the world of detecting, marvelling at her magnanimity in helping to prove that her husband's murderer had not, at least, killed his wife. It would hardly look kind to reward her by charging her with an offence which, had the police got things right in the first place, she would never have needed to commit.

'Consider yourself officially reprimanded,' Jameson said to Angela, when he came to tell her that she was not to be prosecuted. 'The super is pretending not to have heard what I told him, but I think we can expect the Mount Street case to be quietly dropped—not that anyone was looking into it too hard anyway after Valencourt died.'

'Thank you,' said Angela. 'I know I don't deserve it, and I'm sure it was all your doing, but I confess it is something of a relief not to have to worry about going to gaol again. Don't think I don't feel guilty about it, though, because I do, and probably always will.'

'If any lie could be justified, I think this one could,' said Jameson.

'I might almost have believed that until I found out that Edgar didn't kill his wife,' said Angela.

'But you didn't know that at the time,' said Jameson. 'He didn't have to do what he did, and you had nothing to do with his death, so perhaps you ought to try and—I won't say forgive yourself, but perhaps try and worry about it a little less.'

He then went away, and Angela was left to her own unsatisfactory reflections.

Meanwhile, Freddy had also been reflecting on sundry matters. He was not a young man generally given to useless self-doubt, and at twenty-two he had the assurance and self-confidence of a man far older. However, he now found himself faced with something of a moral dilemma, for he knew full well that Edgar Valencourt was still alive and in hiding, and yet he had purposely kept the fact from Angela. He had told himself that he had done so because it would upset her to find out the truth, but now it occurred to him to wonder whether that were indeed the case, or whether, in all honesty, he had withheld the news from her because he disapproved of Valencourt and did not want Angela to become entangled with him again. There was no doubt she was better off without him. If the police knew Valencourt was not really dead then they would arrest him immediately, for although he was now known to be innocent of murder, that did not make him a good man, for he had lived a life of crime for ten years or more and there were still many black marks against his name. Surely Angela deserved better than an unrepentant thief?

And yet Freddy could not help thinking about Angela's sudden outburst on the train. It had been so unlike her to admit her true feelings, and he had seen nothing of the kind from her since, but what she had revealed in that unguarded moment had affected him more than he cared to say, and caused him to wonder whether he had done the right thing. After all, who was he to decide what was best for people? Angela was old enough and wise enough to make her own decisions without any interference from him. He did not want her to be made unhappy by his actions—but she was already unhappy, and who was to say whether his actions might not have the opposite effect? It was a question to which he did not know the answer, and he was hesitant to take the risk for fear of doing the wrong thing.

He was still trying to decide what to do when Angela summoned him one morning a week or two later to tell him that all the arrangements for her departure for the United States were now complete.

'Then you've decided to go,' he said. 'As your adopted son I'll miss you terribly, of course, but I can't say I blame you. Life is easier out there, I understand.'

'I don't know about that,' said Angela, 'but I do want to see New York again. It's a splendid city, Freddy. You must come and visit. I'm sure you'd like it.'

'I'll do my best,' he promised. 'But what about Barbara?'

'Barbara is still thinking about it,' said Angela. 'She's staying at the Ellises' for a few weeks, just for the summer holidays, then she's going to come and join me. We've agreed she shall spend a term at school in America, and if she hates it we'll come back to England. I rather think she'll like it, though. I have an apartment near Central Park, and there'll be plenty of room for both of us, and lots of things to do.'

'Marvellous,' said Freddy. 'I should like a place like that—you know, somewhere to run away to whenever I liked.'

Angela was disconcerted, for his remark reminded her of what Barbara had said only a few weeks earlier.

'I'm not running away,' she said. 'It's just there's nothing much for me here any more, so there doesn't seem any sense in staying.'

'Of course,' said Freddy. 'I quite understand. I shall come and see you off, of course.'

'I shall expect it,' said Angela with a smile.

Freddy went out and down into the street, thinking about what had just passed. He set off briskly in the direction of Regent Street, whistling cheerfully, then stopped suddenly, causing a woman who was just then leaving a shop to collide with him heavily. She snapped at him and he begged her pardon and moved out of her way. There was a telephone box on the other side of the street and he regarded it thoughtfully for a few moments, then, making up his mind, crossed the road and entered it. After a moment's hesitation he picked up the receiver and asked to be put through to a number in Chancery Lane.

CHAPTER TWENTY-EIGHT

T HERE WAS A chilly dawn mist over the sea, and Angela gazed at it absently, thinking about the business that lay ahead of her. She had been unable to sleep and had risen early to take a walk on deck, her mind occupied with the many things which needed to be done when she arrived in New York, for although her agent had kept her apprised of developments weekly, she was sure there were things he must have forgotten. It would take several days before she was in a position to speak confidently to a buyer about how the company had been doing, and she did not wish to appear at a disadvantage. Other than a certain trepidation at the thought of resuming her life in America (for now Davie was no longer there to cause her misery she felt it was safe to return), she was feeling really rather pleased with herself. She had acquitted herself well in the de Lisle case, and had had the pleasure of seeing Mr. Gilverson's evident happiness as he thanked her for what she had done. She had met her moral obligations, had owned up to the police, and was no longer in danger of prison. She was leaving a place that no longer held any joy for her, and would before long be able to show her daughter the sights and the attractions of New York. In addition, her friends had thrown a leaving party for her at which they had all behaved quite ridiculously, and she smiled now at the memory, for she had enjoyed it as much as anybody. Yes, she was on the road to recovery now, it was clear enough.

It was a little colder outside than she liked, however. She took one last breath of the fresh sea air and turned to go back inside to her cabin, and at that moment saw Edgar Valencourt standing a few feet away.

'Hallo, Angela,' he said.

She regarded him in silence. Oddly, she felt no surprise. She ought to have known from the start it was all a lie; that he was not dead, for who could kill such a man? He had outwitted the police for more than ten years and had twice eluded the hangman. How was it to be supposed that a mere rabble of thieves could succeed where far better men had failed? And now he had deceived her once again. He had—almost carelessly, as though it were a thing of no moment—stepped forward to save her life, then escaped from prison and faked his own death. For months she had laboured under the almost unbearable weight of the guilt he had caused her, and now here he was, standing before her, again with that careless look about him, as though everything were perfectly normal and the past had never happened. She knew she ought to say something—

express surprise at his appearance—thank him graciously for what he had done, but instead she felt a rage welling up within her such as she had never felt before, and which could not be contained. She drew in her breath and glared at him in something like pure fury.

'You—you *idiot!*' she hissed, with all the venom she could muster, and then to her utter and everlasting horror burst into tears—not a delicate, ladylike sort of weeping, but a succession of great heaving, gulping sobs that shook her entire body and threatened to overwhelm her, as all the feelings she had so ruthlessly forced into submission since last January rose up together and, smashing down the barricades, made one concerted and successful bid for freedom.

It would be difficult to say which of them was the more aghast at this. He took a step back in dismay and glanced over the rail as though contemplating a header overboard to take his chances in the Atlantic, while she flapped wildly almost as though she hoped to take flight, then whirled round frantically several times, looking for help. In the end, she might have given it up and made a bolt for it had he not just then summoned up the presence of mind to hand her a handkerchief. She grabbed it thankfully and buried her face in it, and then someone walked past and she was forced to calm herself.

'I've had a cold,' she said at last with dignity. 'It can take one that way.'

'Oh, yes,' he said fervently. 'The same thing happened to me just last week. They threw me out of the library.'

'You're not dead, then,' she said after a moment, for want of anything better to say.

'No. I'm sorry.'

'Sorry you're not dead? Or sorry you pretended you were?' inquired Angela.

'Whichever you prefer,' he said carefully. There was a pause, then he said, 'I know I oughtn't to have come, but your friend Freddy said he thought you might not absolutely hate me, so I decided it was worth a try.'

'Freddy? Do you mean he knew all along and didn't tell me?' said Angela in great indignation.

'I expect he thought it was for the best,' said Valencourt. 'And I dare say he was right. But I've wanted so much to thank you in person, and I'm afraid I'm selfish enough to do it, whether I ought to or not. Thank you, Angela, from the bottom of my heart. You don't know what it means to me to have been freed of blame after so long.'

'You're quite welcome,' said Angela gruffly. 'It was the least I could do. I'm sorry about Selina, and your father, and everything.'

'So was I,' said Valencourt. 'But one learns over the years not to think too hard about things. I'd quite resigned myself to never convincing anyone of the truth—until you started looking into it. Then I started to hope that you might somehow pull it off.'

'I nearly didn't,' said Angela. 'I was a very reluctant investigator. I'm ashamed to say I was afraid of what I might find out.'

'I can hardly blame you for thinking me guilty,' he said. 'Everyone else did, after all. And we were hardly a normal family.'

'That's true enough,' said Angela. 'I don't think I've ever encountered anyone quite like your father. Even though he's dead, one could still feel his presence hanging over everything in the house—including your brother and his wife. Was he really that vindictive?'

'Oh, yes,' Valencourt assured her. 'Always. Of course, these days a doctor would probably look at him and conclude that he was not quite right in the head, but it's easy to say that with hindsight. At the time we had to live with it.'

'Still, at least you had one person on your side. It was good of your uncle to help you. You ought to think yourself lucky that he had so much patience with you.'

'I do,' he said. 'Charles is a good fellow. He didn't like deceiving you, but for obvious reasons I couldn't let him tell you I was alive while the murder conviction was still hanging over my head. It would have put you in an impossible position. He agreed with me in the end, but he much prefers an honest life.'

'I'm glad,' said Angela. 'I rather liked him—although he looks so very like you it made me feel quite uncomfortable at times.'

'Yes, he does look like me, doesn't he?' said Valencourt thoughtfully. 'And yet, you know, we're not actually blood relations at all. He was married to my mother's sister, and so is really only an uncle by marriage.'

Angela stared at him, thunder-struck, as this sank in and the final piece of the puzzle at last slid into place. To suggest that there was no blood relationship between Edgar Valencourt and Charles Gilverson was nonsense—why, anybody could see the resemblance! But of course, that explained everything. Roger's sudden falling-out with Gilverson, his pinning of the murder on Edgar, his cruelty in telling Evelyn that he knew her son to be guilty—all those things now made sense. Evelyn could not possibly have been happy in her marriage to Roger, and nobody could have blamed her if she had turned elsewhere for comfort. When had Roger realized the truth? Angela remembered the cryptic remark he had made to Mrs. Poynter about having been betrayed and made a fool of. What had he said? That *something* had been there under his nose for years and that he would make them both pay. Angela had assumed that by 'they' he meant Valencourt and Selina, but now she understood that he must have been talking about Evelyn and Charles Gilverson. Had someone mentioned to Roger quite casually the resemblance between Edgar and his uncle? Or had Roger noticed it himself? Either way he had arrived at the same conclusion Angela had herself just reached, and in his rage had thrown Gilverson out of the house. How he must have made his wife suffer for it! Then, only a few weeks later, Selina had told him she was expecting Edgar's child. What a blow it must have been to him, to discover that the girl with whom he was infatuated had not only rejected him but was about to sully the de Lisle blood-line even further! For a man of his temper it must have been too much for him to take. He had strangled her, and seized the opportunity to revenge himself on all those who had crossed him by his actions thereafter. Edgar would hang, Evelyn would suffer silently, and Charles Gilverson would be forced to watch the consequences of his betrayal from a distance. It all made perfect sense, now.

As these thoughts passed through her head, Angela suddenly found the situation unaccountably hilarious, and without meaning to she began to giggle. She laughed and laughed until she thought she would never stop, and then somehow she was weeping again, and so it was agreed between them that perhaps she ought to go and lie down for a while until she felt better. They went inside and Valencourt delivered a still-hiccupping Angela into the capable hands of Marthe, who was so astounded to see him that she stuck a needle hard into her thumb.

'I think she's had a bit of a shock,' he said, then departed in a hurry, quite possibly in search of a stiff drink, leaving Marthe to suck her bleeding thumb, minister confusedly to Angela and exclaim at length in French, for her English had quite deserted her for the moment.

Later—much later—they met again on deck, and talked more about the deaths of Davie Marchmont and Selina de Lisle. Angela was now perfectly calm and collected, and if pressed would have denied unto her last breath that she had ever made such an appalling spectacle of herself, although naturally Valencourt was far too tactful to mention it. They talked of the past, but murder is a sickening enough subject and the dead are beyond help, so it was not long before the conversation turned to the future, and to matters of more pressing interest to the two who had been lucky enough to survive. An idle observer might have noticed that the gentleman seemed to be exercising his powers of persuasion on the lady, and that was certainly the case, although the lady was somewhat resistant.

'I've told you I won't take responsibility for you,' said Angela.

'But you have no choice,' said Valencourt. 'You're already responsible for me. We're responsible for each other. I saved your life and now you've saved mine and we're bound by that whether you like it or not. Look here: in case it's not perfectly obvious, I'm in love with you. It's a damned nuisance—and so are you, quite frankly, given your half-witted taste in husbands. I'd be on a boat to the Argentine now if it weren't for you, and I'd much rather it hadn't happened, but there's not a thing I can do about it so you'll just have to put up with it.'

Angela glared.

'Thank you, Mr. Darcy,' she said with some asperity.

His mouth twitched.

'Yes, well, perhaps I might have phrased that better,' he admitted.

'I think you might, just a little, yes,' she said. 'And yes, it's true—you saved my life and I saved yours, but that means we're square now. The debt is all paid off.'

'Is that the only reason you did it?' he said. 'To pay off a debt of obligation?'

He was looking into her eyes in that way he had. She had always resisted meeting his gaze in the past, but somehow this time she could not. She said, irrelevantly:

'But the police are looking for you.'

'No they're not,' he said. 'Everyone thinks I'm dead. I can start again from the beginning, just as I meant to before all this mess happened.'

'But the more people who know you're alive the more danger you'll be in. You oughtn't to have come,' said Angela.

'That's what Charles said. He thought I ought to keep away from you and go to South America. But I decided it was preferable to come after you and risk getting caught than to spend forever alone and wanting you. Besides, what's life without a little danger? Terribly dull, don't you think?'

'You're not going to steal things any more, though?' said Angela.

'No,' he said. 'That's all over and done with now. I won't deny it was fun, but I shall leave it behind without regret and merely consider it as a sort of reparation for what happened.'

That brought her up short.

'That's not how it works, you idiot,' she said, aghast. 'Just because you were wrongly accused doesn't mean you're allowed to go around taking other people's necklaces to get your own back.'

'No? Then how does it work?' he said. 'I'm afraid my conscience has atrophied a little over the years. I expect it needs some exercise.'

'It certainly sounds like it,' she said.

'Then will you help me, Angela?' he said. 'I'm willing to learn. Please say you will. I promise I'll do my very best.'

She wanted to answer, just as she always had, that the workings of his conscience were no business of hers, but she could not, for she was no longer sure it was true. He was right: after what had happened there was a connection between them that would be difficult to break—and did she even want to break it? Her head had always told her that she ought to keep far away from him, but it had no chance of victory against her heart, which *would* do exactly as it pleased regardless of what was right. Perhaps it was time to give up the struggle and admit that she had no power to stop it.

'I don't know,' she said feebly at last.

He was still regarding her earnestly.

'I'd like to try and be a better man,' he said. 'I can do it without you, but I'd much rather not. All these months I ought to have been thinking of what it might mean not to have the threat of the noose hanging over my head. I ought to have been making plans for a new life abroad, with new people to meet and new things to do. But instead I've thought of nothing but you. Every time you came to see Charles I bored him silly afterwards with questions about what you'd said, and how you looked, and all the time I was wondering whether you ever thought about me. Eventually I was forced to the conclusion that you didn't, and I was quite resigned to letting you go, but then Freddy came and told me he thought you were unhappy. That's when I determined that I'd try and make you happy again if I possibly could. Will you let me try, darling? We've both had a bad time of it, but we can make one another happy if you'll only say yes—I'm quite certain of it.'

There are many worse things in life than to receive a declaration of love and a promise to reform from a charming and handsome man, however dubious his past activities, and Edgar Valencourt at his most persuasive was a difficult man to resist. The soft-hearted Angela was not proof against any of it, of course. By now she could not have torn her gaze away even if she had wanted to, and she was trying valiantly to prevent herself from sinking, but to no avail. His eyes held hers and asked the question. Slowly, hesitantly, she nodded, and he smiled, satisfied.

They stood for a while at the rail, looking out to sea. He took her hand, and she hesitated but did not protest. Then gradually his arms stole around her, and again she did not object, for after many months in which she had struggled with her own unworthiness, it was very pleasant at last to feel that here, at least, was someone who did not disapprove of her—and in fact showed every sign of liking her very much. One thing was still unresolved, however.

'Forgive me,' she said.

He knew immediately what she meant.

'My darling girl, there's nothing to forgive,' he said. 'I meant you to do it.'

'I know, and I hated you for it,' said Angela. 'But not as much as I hated myself for doing it.'

'Don't feel like that,' he said. 'I have everything to thank you for. You've returned the favour and more. Please don't give it another thought.'

Fine words, but it was not as easy as that. She would never forget what she had done, although she was relieved at his forgiveness. Perhaps one day she would forgive herself too.

'You're too thin,' he said, after a while.

'Oh, so I'm a damned nuisance *and* I'm too thin, am I?' said Angela, who was having to make the strongest effort not to cling to him for dear life. 'I wonder you bothered coming at all.'

'I couldn't resist,' he said softly, his mouth somewhere near her ear. 'You know I'd follow you to the ends of the earth, don't you?'

'That won't be necessary. I'm only going as far as New York.'

'Then that's where I'll go too. You won't get rid of me that easily.'

'So I see,' she said, trying not to smile. 'And yet I tried as hard as I could.'

'You wretched woman, I love you so terribly much,' he said.

'Wretched? There you go again,' she said. 'If you can't be polite then perhaps you ought to stop talking and kiss me instead.'

'What a splendid idea,' he said.

After a few minutes the sun came out and everything began to look brighter, although neither of them noticed. Then people began to come out on deck, and they reluctantly pulled apart and went for a walk.

'You're hurt,' she said, observing that he had a slight limp. 'Then you really were shot.'

'Unfortunately, yes,' he said. 'It was touch and go for a while, but I seem to be as tough as old boots. Besides, I didn't want to give them the satisfaction, not after I'd gone to all the trouble of giving back the brooch to its rightful owners.'

'I'm sorry,' said Angela.

'Don't be. You ought to be glad, because it made me more determined than ever to give up the old life. I've had too many guns pointed at me recently for comfort.'

'I thought it was too much to hope for that you'd had a revelation and suddenly acquired virtue,' said Angela. 'Admit it—you're giving it up because it's more trouble than it's worth.'

'Perhaps,' he said. 'Or perhaps it's just because I've found something I want more.'

She shook her head at him.

'You're quite impossible,' she said, but absently, for her mind was busy marvelling at a most unaccustomed feeling of happiness which the strictest part of her conscience told her she did not deserve. She wavered for a moment then quashed the guilty feeling firmly. She would be good from now on, she thought.

They stopped in a sunny spot and watched idly as another ship passed by in the distance. After a moment he took her hand and examined her wedding-ring.

'Is this valuable?' he said.

'No,' she said in surprise. For a moment she thought he must have forgotten his resolution already, but instead he pulled the ring off and threw it into the sea.

'I don't like it,' he said. 'There—now you're free. Unless you'd like me to get you a new one, of course. What do you think?'

He was looking at her speculatively. Angela stared for a moment, then bridled.

'Mr. Valencourt,' she said severely, 'fate has seen fit to relieve me of the burden of a most troublesome husband. Why on earth should I immediately saddle myself with another and prove you right about my taste?'

'Oh, but look how much we have in common,' he said. 'Our complexions are perfect gallows both. Why, we were made for one another!'

'Don't joke about it,' she said. 'And it's a ridiculous idea. Why, you haven't even a real name to give me—not if you want to avoid being arrested, anyhow.'

'As a matter of fact, I was thinking of taking a nice, respectable American name so as not to stand out when I get there,' he said. 'What do you say to Hieronymus B. Winkelmeyer? It has a certain ring to it, don't you think?'

'Don't you dare!' exclaimed Angela, outraged. 'If you do, I shall never *speak* to you again, let alone marry you.'

'All right then,' he said. 'I shall be plain Edgar, just as before, and give myself a suitably English surname. You may as well give it up at once, though,' he added. 'You know I always get what I want.'

'Not this time,' she said. 'On this point I stand firm.'

'We'll see about that,' he said.

Angela changed the subject. It was an absurd notion indeed. What, marry a man with such a past? Yes, he was in little danger from the police now, and had promised to turn over a new leaf, but could he be relied upon to do it? Despite his words, she was not so complacent as to believe that her influence was enough to reform him. She had no doubt he meant what he said *now*, but who could tell what he would do if temptation came in his way? She would do her best to keep him on the straight and narrow path, as she had promised, but there was only so much one woman could do. It was useless to deny she was in love with him, but she was certainly not about to throw away her new-found freedom as easily as that.

They stood in the sunlight, caught up in one another, oblivious to everything around them. Finally all her walls had come down and she had given up resisting him. When all was said and done, whatever his past misdeeds he was no worse than she; and in one way at least he had proved himself the better man with that absurdly quixotic gesture of his all those months ago in court. She could not say whether they had any future together—and she certainly had no intention of binding herself to him in any way—but for now she was content to drink her fill of the happiness he brought, for who knew how long it would last? Perhaps it would end as soon as they arrived in New York, but that would not be for a few days yet, and even a few days were better than nothing. Between the misery of the past and the uncertainty of the future, she would cling to the present and try to preserve it as long as possible. In the end it was all she could do.

NEW RELEASES

If you'd like to receive news of further releases by Clara Benson, you can sign up to my mailing list here: clarabenson.com/newsletter.

BOOKS IN THIS SERIES

ALSO BY CLARA BENSON:

The Freddy Pilkington-Soames Adventures